Dark Sunshine

by Dorothy Lyons

RED EMBERS
DARK SUNSHINE
BLUE SMOKE
SMOKE RINGS
PEDIGREE UNKNOWN

DOROTHY LYONS

Dark Sunshine

Illustrated by Wesley Dennis

A Voyager/HBJ Book
Harcourt Brace Jovanovich
New York and London

ISBN 0-15-623936-1

E F G H

PRINTED IN THE UNITED STATES OF AMERICA

Contents

1. THE LAZY SL RANCH   3

2. BLIND MAN'S POCKET   14

3. FIVE GOOD LEGS   23

4. FINDERS KEEPERS   34

5. TOP HAND   45

6. THE HYLAND COWBOYS   56

7. MEANT FOR EACH OTHER   66

8. BACK STAIRWAY   76

9. LOVE POTION   87

10. SUNNY DAY   98

11. EMPTY POCKET   111

12. BURLAP JOCKEY   120

13. THE WILL TO DO   130

14. SHASTA   140

CONTENTS

15. LIKE A CRIPPLE   151

16. MERRY-GO-ROUND   159

17. WHODUNIT!   168

18. ADDED ATTRACTIONS   178

19. WITHOUT A LEG
      TO STAND ON   188

20. LAST STAR I'VE SEEN
      TONIGHT   197

21. BOOT, SADDLE,
      TO HORSE, AND AWAY!   206

22. THE FORK IN THE TRAIL   215

23. BLYTHE AND SUNNY   226

24. BONUS   237

Dark Sunshine

I: The Lazy SL Ranch

A SELF-IMPORTANT little train, hooting testily, bustled across the lonely Arizona landscape. Passing a cluster of corrals the train slowed down, for a herd of fat red-and-white Herefords was milling around a loading chute that pointed into the air at an empty siding.

The puffing train frightened them backwards despite the efforts of hot, grimy riders who were trying to force them through the gates. One wily steer swerved and would have taken off for his hills of home but a blaze-faced chestnut wheeled as quick as a cat and horse and rider halted the steer's breakaway almost before it started.

The chestnut's lightning turn and the complete co-ordination between horse and rider jerked a whispered "Good!" from the thin-faced girl who watched from a train window.

The rider's hat fell back and disclosed a mop of curls as red as the Herefords themselves and the traveler realized it was a girl about her own age who had won her approval.

Blythe Hyland settled back in her dusty plush seat as she struggled against the bitterness that swelled within her until it hurt. If it hadn't been for that polio bug two years ago she would be looking forward to similar fun on their new ranch, even if it was rough and run down as her father had warned them. She would have been riding and herding cattle like that girl, but now—her eyes sought the outline of her stunted right leg—there was no use even thinking about it.

But she did, of course, and her thoughts milled around as rebelliously as the steers. After all the years she had wanted a horse of her own, hoped that her folks would move back to a ranch, now they were doing it. What difference would it make to her? Blythe remembered how her brothers—Dan, the eldest, and Chris, next younger than herself—had been speechless with excitement when the Hylands broke the news to their children. Even Amy the baby had squealed with delight while Blythe had sat in apathetic silence. Then she had realized that her mother and father were anxiously awaiting her comment. Despite her own hurt Blythe had wanted to say something that would make them feel better, and not until too late had she realized she had made bad matters worse by saying, "That's dandy—that's fine. It'll be wonderful for all of you."

"Red Rock next stop! Red Rock next!" The conductor's impersonal voice cut through Blythe's thoughts, spared her recalling the pain in her parents' eyes at her thoughtless words that as much as said she didn't intend to like the ranch.

Blythe leaned over and felt around under the double seat for her crutches but straightened up when the conductor paused to speak to the weary trio.

"We won't pull in for a few minutes yet, Mrs. Hyland. Just thought I'd give you plenty of warning. I know folks get pretty well spread around on a long trip like this."

Blythe's eyes turned toward the window again and she watched the flying Arizona scenery. A distant range of mountains rimmed the saucer-like valley that seemed barren until a closer look proved it was covered with bunch grass and dotted with mesquite, greasewood, and cactus with an occasional tuft of cottonwoods along a dry creek bed.

"Miserable-looking country. I hope our ranch isn't like this," she thought to herself. "How does a self-respecting cow ever eke out an existence in such country?"

Her father's earlier advice re-echoed to answer her in his absence. "Don't look at the land to see whether it's good for cattle, Blythe. Look at the cattle themselves. They'll tell you better than anything if it's any good—unless it's overstocked, of course."

Pictures of the fat red steers paraded through her mind to reassure her. Blythe turned her attention to her seven-year-old sister who bounced around like a monkey on a stick, her taffy-colored braids flapping wildly across her shoulders that were just beginning to lose their baby roundness. In spite of her childish ways there was a little-old-lady air about her that became understandable when she bent lovingly over her family of dolls. She was just a little mother, a smaller edition of Mrs. Hyland.

"I wonder if the truck with Dan and Chris and Daddy's horse will be in Red Rock when we get there."

"Of course, dear," Mrs. Hyland assured her youngest. "The man in San Diego told your father it would come in sometime during the night and be ready to follow us to the ranch."

"Suppose Daddy isn't there to meet us?" Amy persisted.

"Oh, stop being silly, Amy. You act as though he'd come down here to get ready for us a year ago instead of a week."

The clatter and grinding of wheels grew suddenly louder as the door to their coach was thrown open and the conductor poked his head in.

"Red Rock! Red Rock!"

Mrs. Hyland straightened her hat, smoothed Blythe's collar, tweaked Amy's skirt with excited fingers.

"You sit still, girls, and I'll go out and send the menfolks in to get our bags and things. Don't try to stand up, Blythe, until the train has stopped. It might jerk you off balance."

"I won't," her daughter promised calmly. "Take it easy, Mom; the train takes on water here so we've got plenty of time."

"There they are! There they are!"

Amy had been kneeling on the seat, her nose pressed against the car window, but she jumped up in excitement. Her knuckles rapped on the glass and she waved furiously at her father and brothers who hurried along beside the slowing train. Blythe leaned toward the window and waved too, but soon settled back, her hands holding the crutches upright in front of her, her purse in her lap.

The train jerked to a halt and Amy scooted ahead to meet

the others at the door. Blythe beckoned and pointed out their things before hoisting herself onto her crutches.

"Need any help, honey? Wait a minute 'til I snake these bags out of here and I'll give you a hand."

"I'm all right now, Dad, but I'll need you for the steps."

His hand grasping a suitcase, Mr. Hyland watched her laborious progress down the aisle and his face reflected the pain that gripped his heart. Instead of the vital, laughing daughter he had once known, he saw a thin listless girl whose pale face made her shadowed blue eyes enormous. Her very hair seemed different and hung down straight and dispirited without any trace of the life and light it had once had. Her thin shoulders bent over the crutches and she actually seemed smaller than she used to be.

"Those crutches are too short! She shouldn't have to lean over so far!" flashed through his mind as he seized an armful of bags and boxes and bundles with more fury than the task warranted, yet when it was Blythe's turn he was all tenderness. He picked her up in his arms and set her on her feet on the station platform.

"There we are, folks. How do you like your new country?"

As if to give them an unobstructed view the train tooted its farewell and pulled out, revealing a sun-drenched plain that shaded from a white glare in the foreground to yellows and reds as the land rose to a distant range of haze-blue mountains. Station activity buzzed on while the half dozen Hylands stood and looked about them, much as a pioneer family might have surveyed a possible site.

Typical rancher was stamped so indelibly on Tyler Hyland

that during his city days just ended he had seemed out of
place working for an aircraft company. He was as long and
slender and lithe as a rope and the crow's-feet that fanned
out from the corners of his blue eyes attested to the miles of
country he had scanned.

Mrs. Hyland, neither as tall nor as slim as her husband,
bubbled with good-natured vitality. On their first ranch, before the growing family prevented it, she had capably filled
the role of extra hired hand whenever necessary. Now her
boundless energies were directed exclusively toward home-
making and caring for the other Hylands.

"What d'ya think of it, Butch?"

Dan looked down at Blythe from his gangling six-foot
height. He grabbed her arm with pretended roughness so
carefully calculated it affected her stance not one bit.

The girl's eyes lighted at the use of a pet name she had not
heard in a long while and she looked at him as if for the first
time. His hair was as yellow and ripply as a wheat field in
bright sun and his eyes reflected the blue of his father's and
the gray of his mother's. He had a calm, unruffled quality that
made him seem more mature than his age, older than just the
year that separated them, but there had always been a special
bond between the two. "We're really twins—although Dan's
a year older," Blythe had once said.

"Looks like it's worth closer examination." She tried for
lightness in her reply which was lost in Chris's cavorting.

"Heigh-ho, Silver," he whooped as he tried to simulate a
prancing horse.

That typified her brother who at twelve years was all ac-

tion and noise, and still changing so rapidly it was hard to say
where he would stop. His tow-headed thatch was one part
blond and two parts sun-bleached, his eyes were hazel one
time, gray another, but his small straight nose and regularity
of feature forecast a satisfactory result.

"Onward to the Lazy SL. Oxcart—I mean truck—now loading."

As he spoke Blythe's father retrieved the luggage that was
spread around them and handed the check stubs to Dan.

"You slip over to the baggage room and get the things that
were sent through on their tickets. I'll come back and help
you with the trunk.

"Mary, you'll have to hold Amy on your lap, I guess," he
told his wife, "so Blythe won't be too crowded. It's not far,
only fifteen miles, though they are fairly rough ones."

"What about eats, Daddy?"

"Never you worry, chick. Why do you suppose I came
down here ahead of you others? All I need now to make the
place perfect is the rest of you."

The baggage was thrown in the back of the pick-up truck
where Dan and Chris loaded themselves for the short ride
back to where the moving van waited. There the boys
transferred and the little cavalcade swung out of town and
up the long slope to the east in the direction of their new
Lazy SL Ranch.

Doubts and misgivings assailed Mr. Hyland as he led his
family toward the new home which must be theirs for better
or for worse now that he had put all his savings into it. Maybe
he had been wrong to buy it without Mary's once-over, but
she had told him to go ahead. Good buys don't last indefinitely.

His womenfolk too rode in silence, Mrs. Hyland wondering if the house was as bad as Ty made out, Amy concerned over the safety of her dolls in back and Blythe hardly knowing what she thought. With their new home so near her curiosity had perked up a little but it had a hard pull against the apathy that had held her since her illness.

Any possible silence was well filled by the rattling and jouncing of the truck as it bumped along over the road that was good only for short stretches between longer stretches of teeth-jarring roughness. Two small ridges were crossed, revealing an immense valley that extended for miles northward and more miles to the south. Like a white string that had been dropped carelessly, their road dipped down into the flat land and wound across it.

They topped one small hill that from the top of the pass had gone unnoticed and Mr. Hyland stopped the truck. He made a sweeping gesture off to the right.

"Ladies, meet the Lazy SL."

"The ranch, Ty? Where?" Mary Hyland squinted into the glare in an effort to locate habitations.

"Over there almost at the foot of that knob. See the light brown dots?"

His finger jabbed at the air as he strove to direct their gaze. Dan and Chris had jumped out of the van as it stopped behind and whether or not they could really see the ranch, they said they did.

"There's Mexico." Again Mr. Hyland's arm swept out farther to the south and his family looked with interest into the next country.

"Doesn't look any different," Chris decided disappointedly. "Are there smugglers and rustlers and stuff over there?"

"There are if you believe what you read in wild west stories"—his father laughed—"but I wouldn't count on it. Just other ranchers trying to make a living the same way we are. Well, here we go on the home stretch!"

The brown dots soon became visible to the others and grew larger and larger. Once the truck had to stop while some red-and-white cows lumbered across the road.

"Are they our cattle, Daddy?" Amy wanted to know.

"No, they belong to our neighbor, Mr. Russell, who is only ten miles away."

In a few minutes they rattled across a cattleguard—several rails spaced parallel to each other across a pit so that stock is afraid to cross but cars can.

"Now we're on the Lazy SL. Does it look any different?"

"Yes, much nicer." Mrs. Hyland squeezed her husband's arm encouragingly.

Another period of silence followed as each looked over their acres. A fence sprang up on the right and ran alongside the road for a quarter of a mile before it turned and pointed toward a cluster of low buildings.

"Horse pasture on right, main ranch house and outbuildings straight ahead," Mr. Hyland intoned with the accents of a professional guide.

"Main ranch house" was a rather grandiose term for so modest a structure. It was long and low and, in fact, Mrs. Hyland decided it must have originally been two small buildings that were later connected by a newer kitchen and service porch.

The construction material was adobe, native clay made into blocks and sun-dried, with wood used for window and door frames, and a porch across half the front that gave the building a droll look. As in all adobes, the windows were small and deep since the walls were thick.

"It doesn't look too bad from the outside. Let's have a look at the inside."

"It's terrible." Blythe's father groaned as her mother stepped to the door. "I've done what I could but it hardly dented the dirt. The junk that was in there—all over the place in fact—is beyond belief. But see for yourself, Mary."

"Phew! I see what you mean!" she exclaimed after a short tour. "Why, I don't even want our furniture brought in here until we get the place cleaned up. Basically it's all right though; and there's nothing the matter that hot water and soap and paint won't cure. There's no time for the latter but scrub it out we can. Come on, young ones. We've got a heap of working to make this house a home."

"I'll help, Mama. What can I do?" Amy volunteered.

"Let's see. How about unpacking some dishes? We'll pretend we're camping out for a while and eat and sleep outdoors 'til the house is clean."

"Sleep outside, Mom? Jeepers, that ground looks awful hard," Chris said dubiously.

"We'll set the beds up outside, goon. It won't rain here for weeks."

"Come on, boys, we'd better get the van unloaded so the driver can start back—and your mother can get to her cleaning supplies. Can't have anything lazy around here but the name."

Mr. Hyland glanced sharply at Blythe, hoping that she too would want to take part in their joint undertaking, but she watched the others impassively. If she noticed his jibe, she felt that she was exempt.

II: Blind Man's Pocket

THERE, I'll bet old Sam Licona would never recognize the place now!"

Mrs. Hyland stood in the center of the living room and surveyed the scene much as a general might look at the site of a victorious battle. No evidence remained of the Hylands' fight, however, except the sparkle that soap and water and elbow grease could leave.

"One of the few advantages the pioneers had—and didn't realize—was not having to work for three days to clean up somebody else's dirt," she added.

"Yes sir, I'll bet those Liconas never threw away anything, just stacked it in the nearest corner." Dan touched his back tenderly at the memory of the innumerable trips he had made to the growing pile of debris behind the barn.

"Well, you never can tell when something will come in handy," Chris said warningly.

"Oh, you! You've got the soul of a scavenger," his mother said with pretended scorn. "If I'd listened to you, we'd still have all that stuff in here on the off chance it might be useful some time."

"Mary, you've accomplished a miracle." Her husband whistled admiringly. "I'd hoped the place could be made livable but I never thought you could make it so much like home."

"Why not? It's a fine big room with a fireplace and once it was brushed down and washed all we had to do was move our own furniture in from the yard. That's what makes it seem like home."

All six Hylands had picked a favorite spot on chair or studio couch or floor to appreciate the change they had accomplished, and while it was the living room they looked at, each one knew that the remainder of the house was just as clean now too. The allotment of bedrooms had worked out nicely. Their parents had wanted the one toward the barn that had its own outside door and the boys had settled for the small room at the rear, leaving the bright, airy one behind the living room for Blythe and Amy.

Though their long move had permitted each one to bring only the dearest possessions there was enough to make it seem like home. Amy had her family of dolls, Blythe her favorite books and the battered old accordion that sounded like a Steinway grand when coupled with her own lilting voice. Chris treasured his rock collection above all else and had Dan wanted to leave behind his chest of tools, each one of which was a particular friend, he would not have been allowed to do so.

"What's next now, Dad? Do we brush the cobwebs out of the barn and wash it down too?" Dan looked whimsically at his father.

"Oh, no, I think I'll have you sweep and dust the range. Don't want the cattle getting dirty, you know! But seriously, now that we have a comfortable place to live, we'll have to get busy on the outside work. At first we'll concentrate around the barn and corrals, but we'll soon have to round up and brand the calves and cut out the steers we want to sell. Once a day you kids better saddle up the ranch horses and ride around awhile to get used to it again, so you won't be so sore you can't sit down after the round-up."

"What about yourself, Pop? The mantel's hardly tall enough for you to use as a table!"

"Don't you worry about me, small fry. Those Sunday rodeos I used to ride in weren't just for fun—they kept my roping arm and eye sharp. Kept Inkspot fit too."

"Let's have a ride now, kids. Come on, Blythe, you can ride old Dick. He looks safe as a hobbyhorse. Amy, you can ride behind me." Chris had things all arranged.

"No, thanks, Chris. I'll stay and help Mother get supper ready. You'll all be hungry when you come in."

"Oh, come on, Butch. You know the doc said it would be all right." Dan had caught a look of longing in his sister's eye before her hand unconsciously dropped to her right leg. "I'll put a lead rein on Dick and he can't possibly do anything—even if he wanted to and I'm sure it's the last thing he'd dream of."

Mr. and Mrs. Hyland fairly held their breaths during the exchange, for uneasy as they would be to have Blythe try to ride it would be worth the risk to shake her out of such passive acceptance of her handicap. Her father flashed a warning look at Mrs. Hyland which she knew meant, "Don't urge her. Sooner or later the time must come."

"OK then. Amy, you rate a horse of your own this time. Let's go." Dan assumed command as the three hurried off.

Mrs. Hyland bustled about the kitchen giving Blythe whatever sitting-down tasks she could. The sound of horses' hoofs drew near only to fade away as the three rode out the drive and turned eastward. Blythe's poised attention told her mother that she had listened until the last hoofbeat faded into silence.

"Why didn't you go, honey? Riding's easier than walking, once you get the knack of it again. You know the doctor says you need some outdoor exercise. You won't want to sit in the house all the time—not with thousands of acres around you to be explored."

"They probably don't look much different from the acres right in front of the door. The potatoes are peeled. Want me to do the vegetable now?"

Her mother accepted the bald change of subject, as indeed she must unless she wanted to make an issue of Blythe's activities. Supper was ready to be dished up before the mounted Hylands returned full of chatter about their surroundings. Their meal was enlivened with enthusiastic descriptions of the fine cattle by Dan, the interesting geological formations by Chris and the darling baby calves by Amy.

They bombarded their father with questions about the boundaries, the cross fences and so many other details he scarcely had time to eat his meal. Mrs. Hyland too asked her full quota since this was the first chance she had had to think beyond what household chore must be done next. Finally Mr. Hyland laid down his napkin in exasperation.

"It's my fault, I suppose, for not having told you more about the ranch, but I'm paying for it now. Just let me eat my supper and afterward I'll brief you on the Lazy SL from A to Z. Come to the living room as soon as dishes are done."

After that announcement Mr. Hyland was allowed some measure of peace in which to finish his meal although its pace was considerably quickened. Blythe, of course, had had no part in the questioning but she had paid close attention to both queries and answers. Her mother nudged her father at the alacrity with which the girl hobbled into the living room and chose a spot close to her father's armchair.

As soon as the others had dried the dishwater off their hands and put away the last dish they trooped into the living room. Mr. Hyland held a long cardboard tube in his hand from which he took a roll of heavy paper and spread it before them.

"This is a surveyor's map of the Lazy SL that will give you a sort of bird's-eye view of the ranch. I've always found it easier to visualize an area once I've seen a map of it.

"Here we are at the home place on the southwestern edge of the small 'home pasture.' Farther south here is the 'south pasture' that extends clear to the border which is itself part of our line. Back there"—his finger moved southeast on the map—"is the 'holding pasture' and along the far eastern edge is the largest of them all, the 'east pasture' which runs right up to that range of mountains." Mr. Hyland pointed through the window to a distant row of mountains that were purple against the evening sky.

"Whew, Pop, how many acres did you say we have here? Must be a whopping big place!"

"Fourteen thousand acres is the size of the ranch but it isn't all ours yet, you know."

"Jiminy, it won't take us long to pay for it with the hundreds of cattle we can run on fourteen thousand acres. It'll be ours in no time."

"Easy, son. It won't be as simple as it sounds. Remember that range such as this can support only about one cow per hundred acres as an average—and if we had a bad year of light rains even that would be overcrowding."

"Hm-m, then a hundred and forty cows is our peak," Chris said thoughtfully, but he concluded sturdily, "Well, even that's pretty good."

"Sure it is. We'll do all right but it'll mean a lot of hard work."

"Dad, what's this little dent here in the line? Looks funny."

At Dan's question Mr. Hyland bent closer to the map and scanned it in silence for a moment.

"Oh, that! For a minute you had me stumped, but now I remember. Sam Licona told me that he and Mr. Williams had made a deal on that. The line fence went right through the middle of a big wash and during heavy rains the fence was always being taken out by the rush of water, so he gave that little hunk to Williams who in turn gave him this little chunk. It was a poor trade though."

Mr. Hyland's finger shifted to another spot on the map where instead of a dent there was a hump in the otherwise straight boundary.

"Another creek, Daddy?" Amy asked to take part in the meeting.

"Yes and no, punkin. It's a deep slit into that range of mountains—matter of fact its only entrance was on our land through a narrow gap cut out during thousands of years by the tiny stream. From the cliffs above you can see it's a little Garden of Eden—or so I'm told—with lush grass, its own little spring, even a miniature hill in the center—really just a knob."

"It sounds beautiful, but why the past tense?"

"Because shortly after Licona and Williams traded there was an extra wet winter and a landslide came along and sealed up the entrance so nobody can get in now at all."

"What about the spring? Did the valley fill up with water?" Chris, the practical, asked.

"No, the water just disappears into the rocks and dirt that block the opening. At least so they tell me. I've never really seen the place myself. It used to be well-known to all the prospectors and hunters who roamed through here—they called it Blind Man's Pocket."

"It's a shame to have it cut off from our range," Dan said thoughtfully. "It ought to support another cow or two, shouldn't it, Dad?"

"Yes, or more. I figure it is probably an old crater with rock strata that lead clear deep down. It must have more underground springs than the one that comes to the surface for the grass is always good. Licona said it ought to be waist-high by now."

They were all silent, their imaginations caught by the idea of a Garden of Eden all their own, even though inaccessible. The women pictured a green meadow carpeted with flowers

and watered by a tinkling brook; the men visualized it dotted
with fat cattle.

" 'Blind Man's Pocket,' " Blythe mused. "Did a blind man
ever live there?"

"That I wouldn't know, hon. Probably it's just because it's
a blind lead. Now," he looked around him, "are there any
more questions? If not, the meeting stands adjourned."

Adjourned the meeting might be but the conversation was
not and the ingenious Hylands vied with each other propos-
ing improvements for the ranch to make it pay off better, to
add to their comfort and ease of operation. Amy capped it
all with her suggestion, and then was a little hurt at the
hilarious reception it met.

"Daddy, Daddy, let's just keep the cows that have twin
babies so our herd will grow twice as fast."

"That's my little businesswoman," he approved when he
could control his voice. "Do you have any suggestions,
Blythe?"

He turned to his other girl who sat staring out the window
at a silver-dollar moon ballooning up from behind the shadowed mountains.

"How far is it, Dad?" she asked dreamily as she felt his attention on her.

"How far-fetched, you mean?"

"No, how far to Blind Man's Pocket? Sometime when
you're going that way take me along with you."

A tightness in his throat prevented her father from answering until a lusty pinch from his wife jarred his speech loose.

"Quite a ways, Blythe. It'd have to be on horseback. There
are too many steep washes to get the truck through."

"Yes, that's what I mean, horseback. Do you think I could make it?"

"Why, sure you could, hon, but not from scratch. Better do a little practicing first, but you'll have plenty of time. I can't get away until after the round-up and branding. The sooner we get those steers to market while prices are high, the surer we'll be of eating next winter."

For one wild moment he was ready to throw other plans to the wind, anything to get Blythe interested in something, but his usually good judgment prevailed.

"That's all right," she assented easily. "It'll give me time to get the hang of it again."

"Fine, you can help us with the branding. We'll need all the hands we can muster for that. You and Dick will be just the ticket for moving the stock in and out of the round corral for us."

"Bedtime, young ones. Tomorrow's another day," Mrs. Hyland said quickly lest Blythe have a chance to change her mind. "Breakfast at six."

"Six! Ma, has the sun teched you already?" Chris wailed.

"No, it's to make sure it doesn't tech the rest of you. This is siesta country, so you get up early and do as much as you can before lunch in order to stay out of the sun during the hottest part of the day. You'll notice even the animals are smart enough for that too. Six I said and six it is. Now git!"

III: Five Good Legs

"You won't let go of the lead rein, will you?"

"Of course not, Butch. Cross my heart," Dan promised with appropriate gesture. "Now up with you."

By the next morning Blythe regretted her hasty decision to try riding again although the thought of Blind Man's Pocket still drew her like a magnet. During her wakeful night she had examined her motives with the honesty that darkness and solitude permitted. Alluring though the little valley sounded, she decided that alone could not have been strong enough to shake her from a decision she had intended should last her lifetime, and so she concluded it must have been the name that drew her. "Blind Man's Pocket" stirred feelings of interest and sympathy, but whatever the cause by morning Blythe would have welcomed any sound reason for changing her mind.

"Are you sure Dick's absolutely sure-footed? If he stumbled in a badger hole I'd go off on my neck—or my leg."

"He's as sure-footed as a mountain goat. But you find out for yourself. Dad, you steady his head and I'll swing Butch into the saddle."

Only the three of them were present since Mrs. Hyland had set Amy and Chris at indoor tasks—on purpose, Blythe realized gratefully.

"We-e-l-l—" She exhaled slowly, making one last-minute effort to gather her courage, but before her tongue could finish the last "l" Dan picked her off her crutches and set her in the saddle.

"There you are, Butch. Just swing that leg over the pommel and you're in!"

Blind terror swept through Blythe as she left the ground and she froze immobile, sitting sidesaddle, her hands gripping pommel and cantle desperately. Forgotten was her last-ditch hope that once they saw how useless it was for her to try to ride again they would leave her alone, forgotten the lure of Blind Man's Pocket, forgotten everything but her frantic desire to get safely back on the ground.

"Wake up, Sis. Get that leg over there," Dan prodded with gentle raillery. "See, Dick's the perfect gentleman and won't make a move until you're ready."

"Don't hurry her, Dan. Let her take her time."

From a distance Blythe heard her father's low-voiced advice and she almost begged him to make Dan set her down again. The two men waited patiently to give her time to get used to her new situation, but it was Dick himself who resolved the crisis. He was apparently unused to such inaction

and though he was too well-mannered to move until com-
manded, he did turn his head around and Blythe met the soft
look in his wise brown eyes.

The knot of terror in her heart slowly relaxed and she was
able to feel the strength in Dan's arms that were still around
her waist. He sensed the change in her and looked up questioningly.

"All set now? Ready to shift? One, two, thre-e-e!"

Once again, after what seemed like a lifetime, Blythe was
sitting on a horse and the world looked better immediately.
She was suddenly surprised to realize that Dan had put her
up from the wrong side but his next words proved he had a
motive.

"After a while you can learn to mount from the left side
on your good leg, but at first it looked easier to get you on
from this side so it'd be your good leg that you swung over
the horse's back. There now, how do you feel?"

"Pretty good—considering," the girl admitted sheepishly.
"Heigh-ho, Silver, awa-a-ay— at a slow walk, please."

"That's my girl," her father said with pride. "You'll see
Blind Man's Pocket in no time."

Surprisingly enough it didn't seem nearly as unattainable
as it had but a few minutes earlier and thinking of it made
the horse's first few steps easier until Blythe could settle into
a more comfortable position. Her eyes were fixed on Dick's
head as it swayed to his careful walk. Slow though it seemed,
the ground flowed past swiftly—swiftly, as she contrasted it
with her own halting progress.

Blythe flashed a smile at Dan who rode close beside her,

his hand holding the lead rein attached to Dick's bit. The early morning sun warmed her face, a light breeze touched her hair as they covered the ground faster than she had ever hoped to again. She was earth-bound no longer. The world was hers and the thrill of that realization was to stand out in her memory as the most significant moment of her whole life.

"Now I have five good legs instead of only one, Dan. It's wonderful!"

"That it is, Sis, and you'll soon be able to go along with us—or by yourself. You'll learn the trick of mounting without help."

"Sure I will. After all, it's my best leg that I'll pull myself up with."

"There's one thing I want to impress on you, Butch." Dan's use of her special nickname impressed Blythe more than his words. "Don't pay any attention to that stuff about not 'pulling leather.' If you feel yourself going, you grab for that saddle horn and hang on like a puppy to a stick. It's better for a horse to have you stay on, however you do it, than go off. Of course, with Dick it probably doesn't make any difference but there are horses that, once they find their riders are not supermen, just might get into bad habits. And as for yourself, you know how important it is to stay right side up with care. Savvy?"

"Me savvy," Blythe agreed humbly. "I'm sure my instincts would win over my pride anyway. I don't want anything to happen that will prevent my going on riding for years and years and years."

They had circled the house and barn and corrals once and

Dan wisely decided to end Blythe's trial run on a high note. He reined up to the backyard.

"Do we have to stop so soon?" the girl asked with disappointment in her voice.

"We sure do. Don't want to tire you too much the first time, but don't worry, I'll see that you get a ride every day, Sis."

Though Blythe's take-off had been in the comparative privacy of only half the Hylands, she returned like a conquering hero into the arms of the whole family, including all the cats and Super, the dog. Everyone's excited enthusiasm showed Blythe how much it meant to them all—almost as much as it did to her.

Thenceforth no matter how busy or tired Dan might be, Dick was saddled and led up to the backyard where Blythe was put aboard. Even she was surprised by the ease with which she adjusted herself to her new, or renewed, activity. The first few times had hurt her leg occasionally but this, she decided, was because she was trying to grip with her legs as she once had. As soon as she changed her style of riding to one of balance, the pain left her.

The worst drawback was always having to have either her father or Dan there to lift her into the saddle. Wanting something badly enough, she learned, is the next thing to gaining it, and before she had graduated from riding on a lead rein she began trying to mount unassisted. Dick stood like a statue wherever he was put and Blythe tried climbing on from boxes, from blocks of firewood, even from the ground when nothing else worked out satisfactorily, but the real solution was found by chance.

One morning Blythe had stayed in the kitchen to help her mother until Dan brought the horse up to the backyard and, not seeing Blythe, he led Dick over by the low, unrailed back porch.

"Sis, come over here to the corner and see how this is for getting on," he directed when she pushed through the screen door.

Blythe hobbled to the outside corner of the porch as directed and one move led to the next. She dropped her left crutch and put her weight on the right one to steady herself while she put her left foot and weight in the stirrup nearest her. This meant she had to let go of the second crutch to grasp the horn which left her standing in one stirrup, her bad leg dangling unsupported.

"Now see if you can't swing it over, Butch. Try hard!"

As if hypnotized by Dan's intensity Blythe contracted the muscles in her right leg and swung mightily but ineffectually. Her leg flopped back to the perpendicular.

"That was fine, Butch! Try it again," Dan encouraged.

Tiny dots of perspiration jeweled Blythe's face, not alone from the physical exertion but also from the mental effort as she willed her right leg over Dick's back. Again she tried and this time she would have made it but for her truant toe that dragged and caught on the horse's rump until a lightning push by Dan made her leg complete the arc and swing down by the offside stirrup.

"Good girl. That was super. Next time you'll be able to make it yourself or I miss my guess."

Dan was as thrilled as she was by her progress and Mrs.

Hyland who had been hovering inside the screen door hurried out with her congratulations.

"Good for you, honey. You're a brick."

For a moment Blythe was too breathless from exertion and excitement to do more than sit in her hard-won perch, but her flashing smile was answer enough. Dan mounted and started out the driveway.

"Hey, haven't you forgotten something? Where's the lead rein?" Blythe called in sudden panic.

"I don't think you need it any more. Old Dick's feelings have been hurt by our using it and I think you'll make faster progress without it. Come on and try it solo for a while and then if you still want it, I can snap it on easy enough."

Blythe's new taste of freedom was sweet and made her greedy for more. Not many rides later she tired of walking and was eager for a faster pace, so Dan obligingly put his horse into a jog trot and Dick followed suit. It took but a few steps of this to show Blythe that, for the present at least, the trot was not for her.

"Whoa, Dick. Whoa, Dan," she chattered indiscriminately to her horse and her brother. "Phew! That's not good. Guess I'll have to be content to just dog along at a walk. Jeepers! That trot's real punishment!"

Dan pulled his horse back to a walk and they rode in silence. Forgotten was her first thrill at Dick's fast steps, and disappointment bit deep into Blythe that she must be content with only a walk. Dan too felt her mood with the sixth sense they had for each other. He turned in his saddle and unsnapped the lead rein from the ring where it hung.

"A canter's lots easier riding, you know. Want to try one on the rein?"

His daring suggestion made Blythe catch her breath until she reasoned that in reality it was safe enough. With the lead rein Dick couldn't do anything out of line and there was no denying that any canter is easier to sit than a trot. And she could always hold on to the horn.

"Why not!"

At her signal Dan lifted his horse into a lope, Blythe touched Dick with her one good heel and, veteran cow ponies that they were, the two horses stepped out in a rocking-chair rhythm that was as exhilarating as a ride on a roller coaster. Sagebrush and mesquite flew backwards as if borne on a wind and once again Blythe savored riding's ultimate thrill.

It seemed there were no drawbacks at all to the pace for its regularity made balancing easy for Blythe, nor did her right leg protest at the extra motion. Only the lead rein that stretched between the horses remained to remind Blythe of her disability, but nothing as unimportant as a strip of leather could bother her then and her mind told her that in time that too would be discarded.

At the supper table that evening, as soon as Blythe had satisfied her new-found appetite, she told of her most recent progress. Her eyes sparkled as she talked and there was a deeper, more natural color in her face than had been there in many moons.

"How soon do you think we'll have the round-up, Dad? I can hardly wait to ride over and peek down into Blind Man's Pocket."

Her father's mind was not on her question as he stared at the girl, changed almost as if by the wave of a fairy god-mother's wand.

"Why, Blythe," he exclaimed suddenly. "You've got a freckle."

"Where? Where? Where?" she chorused with the rest of the Hylands.

"Right the-r-e." His finger tapped the tip of her nose with a tenderness that went back to his earlier thoughts.

"I'll have to wear my hat more," she said decisively, un-aware of the silent hosannas the others were singing. "But, Dad, when can we ride over?"

"Are you up to it so soon? That's a long ride and you haven't ridden half that far yet."

"No, but I will have by the time you're ready. Round-up and branding and shipping will take several days, won't it? Surely you can't go now?" she asked in sudden anxiety lest she miss out after all.

"Well, I could. I've decided to postpone the branding a few days as several cows I'd about given up have calved and they ought to be a little older and stronger for their roles."

"What about your wanting to sell the beef cattle now? Will—will—" Dan hardly knew how to ask what he was worrying about.

"Oh, we'll go on eating if that's what's bothering you, and the market seems to be holding steady."

"Then I won't get to go after all?"

The disappointment in his sister's voice was too much for Dan and he came up with another suggestion.

"Sis can ride quite a ways, Dad, though not as far as the east line. Why couldn't Chris and I go on ahead, leading Dick and Inkspot and you two come along in the pick-up. We'll meet you at the turn-off and Butch could make it from there. Couldn't you?"

She flashed him her thanks in one look, at the same time assuring her father that it'd be a cinch under those conditions. This was rather calling his hand but after a quick exchange of glances with Mrs. Hyland he agreed and set the ride for two mornings later.

"Looks like you'll have to stay home with your mother, punkin," he said regretfully to his younger daughter. "The Liconas should have had the foresight to leave four horses with the Lazy SL instead of three. But she'll want company anyway."

"I don't mind, Daddy. I'm making a new dress for my dolly and can prob'ly finish it without any interruptions," Amy agreed primly, borrowing words she had heard her mother use.

"How can I wait? Day after tomorrow I'll see Blind Man's Pocket," Blythe said excitedly.

"So what?" Chris countered.

"Well, I'll have seen it. That's all, but I feel that I *have* to go there!"

The currents of excitement that shot through her were not to be short-circuited by her younger brother's words. Some lodestar was drawing her to the Pocket and though she told herself that they could only peer down from the heights, she pictured herself dancing through fields of daisies, wading in a crystal-clear stream.

"Blythe, 'please pass the butter,' I said—for the 'steenth time."

Again Chris swept away her daydreams but they bided their time and returned that night and the next with their even more colorful cousins.

IV: Finders Keepers

THE RISING sun cast such long, thin shadows it was impossible for them to ever catch up with Dan and Chris and the four horses when they rode away from the barn and turned full toward the black outline of the east range. Blythe waved them off while a flurry of impatience and anticipation danced inside her head.

Where would the sun be when she first peered into Blind Man's Pocket? Blythe shot a calculating glance at its position and reluctantly admitted that it must show much more progress before she could be anywhere near the Pocket. She fidgeted around in a caricature of helping until her mother drove her out of the kitchen with playfully irate advice.

"Go and play your accordion awhile. Maybe that will settle you down."

"Yes, Blythe, do go into the living room and let us get the work done," Amy seconded, "or I'll never get to my sewing."

Taking their broadside hints, Blythe wandered into the living room and, picking up her accordion, she trilled off a few scales before whirling into a fast dance. From that she jigged into an even faster piece. This could not satisfy her feeling of haste so she concentrated on the three rising notes of "fare thee well" which she played faster and faster and faster until the kitchen pair was ready to fare-thee-well her before her right hand crashed down on the keys in one magnificent discord.

"Isn't it about time for us to be going, Dad?"

Blythe had caught sight of her father working in the yard and called her question from the doorway.

"No, they've hardly gotten a start yet."

"I don't know about that. Seems like they've been gone a long time."

"You can still see them. There, on top of that rise down the road."

Blythe looked as directed and true enough, a dark speck moved along the white road and dipped out of sight again. She picked up a book and turned a few pages with supreme disinterest, only to bang it down decisively. Waiting would be easier if she went as far as she possibly could.

"Tell Dad I'll be out in the pick-up," she told her mother on the way through the kitchen. " 'Bye, Amy, don't smother that doll with loving kindness."

Blythe achieved some degree of patience as she leaned back against the torn cushions of the truck, her thoughts miles away in Blind Man's Pocket. A tiny doubt began boring into her mind, warning her of disappointment ahead. No place could ever live up to the magic with which she had endowed that one.

She had just admitted to herself that she had been behaving like a child who still believed in fairy stories when the left-hand door opened and her father slid behind the wheel. Blythe's hopes and dreams flashed up again as bright as a bonfire.

"Promise me, hon, that if you begin to tire you'll tell us in time to turn back before any damage is done."

"Oh, I won't get tired, Dad. Don't you worry about that."

"That's not what I asked. Promise?" he insisted, and his foot did not touch the starter until he had exacted her word. "All right, then, here we go."

Blythe waved excitedly to her mother and Amy who came out on the back steps, nor did her impatience abate during the ride. She perched on the edge of the seat as if to urge the car forward. Her father had timed it well, for when they drew up Dan and Chris were less than a quarter of a mile from the trail's turn-off.

There was a short delay while saddles were checked and the truck's cargo—lunches, canteens, binoculars—was stowed in saddlebags. Dan stepped over to Blythe to lift her on in spite of her proud assertion that she could make it from the running board.

"No need to today. Better save your oomph for the ride," he argued sensibly and swung her up.

The others mounted and two by two the quartet left the road and headed across the open range. Dan's spirits rose to match his sister's and his passable tenor told them they were "Off to see the Wizard, the wonderful Wizard of Oz" from the old movie that had been his and Blythe's favorite. Soon her soprano blended in and they harmonized with their old-time zest and precision. The horses seemed to step along more gaily and Mr. Hyland would gladly have tried to ride around the world if it would keep that lilt in his daughter's voice.

The day warmed up rapidly and by the time the riders had reached the first mountain slopes songs and talk had dwindled to occasional snatches but that was no indication of sagging spirits. Mr. Hyland reined in briefly, dismounted and opened a limp wire gate through the fence.

"Now we're on Williams's property. Better go single file from here on, it gets rough fast. I'll take the lead, then you, Chris, Blythe, and Dan, you bring up the rear. Yell a 'whoa' if you want us to stop."

The horses' heads lowered as they leaned forward for the climb. Blythe admired the care with which Dick chose his footing, for never a loose rock nor treacherous piece of shale did a hoof rest on, and her hand on his shoulder told him of her approval. Topping a low ridge they stopped to breathe the horses and for once Blythe's interest was directed backward at the Lazy SL acres spreading so far behind them they could hardly pick out the tiny dot that already meant home.

Mr. Hyland started on and again the girl kept her attention on the trail, so completely that she looked up in surprise, expecting another rest stop, when her father's sweeping gesture halted them.

"There it is, kids. Blind Man's Pocket. Doesn't look 'as dark as a pocket,' does it?"

From their position on the cliffs the quartet looked down into a sun-drenched circle. A strip of yellow sand and gravel marked the stream bed that started in a clump of bushes and wound lazily across the floor of the Pocket and along the base of the opposite parapet. Once Blythe thought she caught the flash of reflected sunlight from the water. A sprinkling of sycamores and cottonwoods gave the valley a parklike appearance that was further heightened by the meadow grass with its spatter of wild flowers.

"What about that grass, Dad? Something must have happened either to it or your calculations. It sure isn't anywhere near waist-high."

Dan reminded them of Mr. Hyland's prediction which had seemed reasonable enough at the time, but there was no evidence of grass or weeds gone to seed.

"Hrmph! Can't be as much underground water here as I'd expected. Maybe the place isn't such a loss after all."

"There's still grass enough there for two or three cows and their calves though, Pop," Chris said judiciously. "We ought to add it to our range."

"Maybe there's something there eating the grass, deer or— or something," Blythe suggested.

"With wings? No, it must be a matter of water—just as everything in this country is," Mr. Hyland countered. "Well, Blythe, now you're here, is it as wonderful as you'd expected it would be?"

"Ye-es, but it makes me want to get down into it all the more. Is the entrance totally blocked?"

"Totally—unless you had a couple of steam shovels, some bulldozers and a ton or two of dynamite. But come on, let's ride around the rim so we can see it from all angles. Here, Blythe, have a squint at it through the glasses. Makes it seem closer. Sure is a pretty little spot, isn't it?"

The girl swung her horse's head around in order to give her a clearer view and trained the binoculars on the hillock and spring. At the instant she looked, a long, shrill neigh cut the air and Blythe had the sensation that the glasses were wired for sound. Their horses chorused an answer and, while her father and brothers looked behind them for the unseen trumpeter, Blythe was the first to behold it.

Scattering rocks and dirt like chaff, a buckskin leaped the brook and charged to the top of the little hill, bugling a series of equine questions, answers, invitations to the strangers above. The horse's perfection of form and absolute freedom held Blythe spellbound, the glasses glued to her eyes.

"Look! Look! A wild stallion," Chris cried as the others snapped their gaze into the valley.

"A wild mare, you mean, and what a mare," Blythe corrected with the advantage of the binoculars. "Oh, you beautiful, beautiful beauty!"

Fairness made her relinquish the glasses to her father though she continued to strain her eyes to miss not a single detail.

"She looks wild enough," Mr. Hyland agreed, "but I don't think she's a real 'wild' horse. No wild mustang ever had conformation like that. And what a coat! I've never seen a more glorious color on a buckskin."

For an instant she posed motionless on the center pinnacle but she could no more stand still than Robinson Crusoe when

he found the footprint. She wheeled and rushed headlong
down the slope and across the grassy meadow, her black
mane floating on the wind, the bone in her tail straight up so
that the hairs streamed out behind like a banner. Just as she
was about to disappear in a thicket she curved and raced
back to a new vantage point where she again posed, head
thrown up so high there was a straight line from her front
legs up the under side of her neck. A luxuriant black foretop
had parted to show a wide forehead topped by delicate black-
edged ears that flicked back and forth nervously and finally
pointed motionless at her callers.

"█████ Dad, the Liconas left four horses after all," Chris
chortled.

"The Liconas never owned a horse like that, nor any that
she could have come from. She's somebody's stray—but
whose?" he puzzled.

"Her head looks Arabian," Blythe, who had recovered the
glasses, decided.

"Of course! That explains everything. She flew in on a
magic carpet!" Chris cackled and nearly fell off at his own
joke.

"There are Arabians closer than Arabia, short stuff," his
sister aloofly pointed out.

"She does look Arabian at that, you know. That delicate
muzzle and dished profile are dead giveaways." It was Dan's
turn to look through the binoculars. "Let's circle the rim and
see if we can find how she got down there."

They rode back out of sight to detour a rocky prominence
and as they disappeared the mare broke into a fresh series of
whinnies that they thought would never stop.

"She's lonesome as a pup down there and doesn't want us to leave," Dan commented. "Bet she'd do anything for company."

When they reappeared her neighs diminished though she kept abreast of the riders as they circled the edge. From time to time she trotted away in as stylish a trot as was ever seen in a show ring only to come about in a canter and thunder back at a gallop.

"Doesn't she have easy action? Bet that canter wouldn't hurt me a bit," Blythe mused.

"Hurt *you!*" Chris cried out. "She isn't your horse. Why, you—you—"

Luckily he bit off the cruel thing he had almost said, considerably helped by a lusty kick from Dan's high-heeled boot, but Blythe was unaware of anything but the mare. Even Dick was allowed to pick his own course, his own gait, just so long as he kept his rider within view of the beautiful buckskin.

Their circuit completed, no one had seen any place that looked as though a mountain goat, much less a horse, could have descended to the valley floor. At one point they had had to make a wide detour around the arm of a side canyon that led backward from the precipice but Chris had followed the edge around with no luck.

"Then she must have come through the entrance," Mr. Hyland declared.

"Why, sure. Why didn't we think of that before? She could have come in before the landslide and been trapped inside. Otherwise she would have gone out again to find her own kind. No wonder she's lonesome after five years of solitary confinement. By now I'll bet she'd try anything to get out."

Blythe's imagination was on fire reconstructing the buckskin's past.

"It must have been terrifying for her when the landslide happened. But if she had to be trapped any place, she certainly picked a dandy. Dad, do you think there's any chance of getting her out?"

"Very little, chick, and what's the use? Suppose we got her out? We can't prove ownership and somebody else might come along and claim her—and there'd go all our work!"

"That's so," the girl agreed despondently. "But 'finders keepers,' Dad, and she's been grazing on our land for several years. We'd own her for her board bill."

"We'll own her, I guess, until she goes to the Happy Hunting Ground, but much good it will do us. Here's a good big mesquite bush. Let's eat lunch and stretch our legs before we start back."

Mr. Hyland swung off his big black and dropped the reins to the ground. Not until then had Blythe realized how tired she was and she could do nothing until Dan came to lift her off. Her crutches had been left in the truck so, after hopping around a minute or two on her good leg, she stretched out on the ground and the warmth of it soaked up into her tired back and legs.

Lunch was soon finished but Blythe was reluctant to return to the saddle though unwilling to admit it. Dan gathered up the reins of his horse, tightened the cinch and mounted.

"I'll be back in a few minutes. Take it easy, Sis."

She watched him canter off toward the other side of the rim but she soon turned her attention back to the valley and the buckskin. The division of forces above puzzled the mare and she could hardly decide whether to follow Dan's course or stay near the larger group. Actually she did neither, following Dan for a bit, only to wheel and come sweeping back toward them.

Blythe was so enchanted with the mare she felt she could stay there forever and watch her and it seemed that Dan returned almost as soon as he left. The group then remounted and began the long, hot ride home.

"Anyway, I felt all along there was more in the Pocket than its lining," Blythe said with satisfaction. "I knew there was some reason for coming over here."

"Yep, you were right, sister dear," Chris agreed humbly, "and to reward you for your sixth sense, I'll give up all my rights to the mare."

"That's downright magnanimous of you, little brother, especially in view of your certainty that we can never get her out of her prison. Thank you, and thank you again," Blythe accepted drily.

V: Top Hand

ONCE IN an armchair instead of a saddle Blythe found out just how tired she was. As soon as supper was over she went to bed, leaving her door open so that she could join in any talk about the buckskin.

She opened her eyes and sat up to add something to what her father had said about the mare, but it was bright daylight. Amy had come and gone and already she heard Dan and her father working down by the corrals. Blythe closed her eyes and fell back on her pillow to savor her dreams of the buckskin that she had been robbed of by so deep a sleep.

The beautiful mare had just circled her at a gallop, stopped and taken the first step toward her outstretched hand when she heard her mother in the doorway. Loath to banish so beautiful a vision with sunlight, Blythe kept her eyes shut but Mrs. Hyland was not fooled.

"You're awake, lazybones, I can tell by the way your eyelids move."

Her mother sat down on the edge of her bed when Blythe opened her eyes.

"How do you feel after your workout?"

"Wonderful! Just wonderful—if you don't count my being kind of lame and sore. Oh, Mother, but she's a beauty!"

Mrs. Hyland saw the dream in her daughter's eyes but treated it lightly for fear it would build up to further heartbreak.

"She certainly sounds grand. It's too bad she wasn't sired by Pegasus so she could fly out—but then, she belongs to someone else anyway. So how about some breakfast? I'll have it ready by the time you're dressed."

"How'd Amy make out with her dressmaking yesterday?" Blythe asked, returning to reality.

"Just fine, though she almost didn't get the hem put in for worrying about whether styles are going up or down. She's a precise little piece, that one!" Mrs. Hyland laughed fondly.

Blythe was further plunged into reality by her father's statement at lunch.

"Well, day after tomorrow I guess we'll start gathering the cattle. That will take two or three days and by then the calves ought to be ready for branding."

"Can I help, Dad? I'm getting pretty handy," she offered quickly.

"Sure you can, hon. Not on the long rides, but we'll leave

Dick saddled and when you see us bringing in a herd you can get on the other side of the gateway to help turn 'em in."

"Can I, Daddy? A big job like that will require all hands." Amy liked the sound of the phrase she had heard her father use whenever a major project was in the offing.

"That it will, punkin, and I'll have a job all cooked up for you, come branding time, but I'm afraid there won't be a need for your services 'til then."

The boys knew they didn't have to offer their help, it was counted on as part of the plan. They made a great show of getting the kinks out of their ropes and they carried them everywhere they went, even if it was just walking from the house to the barn. Superdog soon learned to give them a wide berth whenever he saw either of them with a coiled lariat, and so their talents were exercised on stones, posts, blocks, or any projection that offered a suitable target.

Round-up preparations completely eclipsed further conversation about the buckskin but could not blot her out of Blythe's memory. She kept recalling each of the mare's superior qualities and contrasting them with patient old Dick. The first ride she had on him after their trip to the Pocket she became very critical of his every move and told him that he fell far short of the buckskin's perfection until a fit of remorse seized her.

"Don't listen to me, Dick, old boy. I'm an ingrate, that's what I am, after the fine care you've taken of me. But she is lovely, and I'll bet you'd like her too—if you ever had a chance!"

Before sun-up the next day the Hyland cowboys rode out on the first day's round-up and the womenfolk were left

with a long day ahead of them as there was little likelihood
of the men bringing in the first group of cattle before late
afternoon. Dick had been haltered and tied in the garage shed
out of the sun to be ready for Blythe but, rather than have
him stand all day under saddle, Mrs. Hyland said she would
get him ready later.

Blythe and Amy took advantage of the time to help their
mother with the mending that had piled up during their moving and settling. Sometime after lunch Mrs. Hyland folded
the last pair of blue jeans with a satisfied sigh.

"There! I'll bet the men haven't done a better day's work
than this. It'll be wonderful if we ever have our own elec-
tricity so I can use my sewing machine again."

"Lights will be nice instead of lamps too, Mama," Amy
added.

"Neither of them is anything compared to an electric re-
frigerator," Blythe stated with no word of denial from the
others, "but we can't complain. We're pretty comfortable
here and we knew we couldn't bring city comforts along."

"Blythe, I think it's about time we got you saddled and
mounted and ready for the fray. Better to have you in your
place too early than too late. My! Wouldn't Ty be mad if
you weren't there to turn 'em and the cattle went right on
past us."

"Boy, I'll say he would. I'd better get going."

Knowing that she had a real job to do made this ride much
more important to Blythe and she pulled her hat on at a
jauntier angle when she got outside. Her mother led Dick
into position by the porch and stood by to help push Blythe's
right leg over Dick's back.

"No, don't help me, Mother. I can make it. I know I can."

For an instant she stood motionless in the left stirrup as she tensed her muscles, her mind, her will for the effort. She made one preliminary swing before an all-out effort that carried her leg up like a pendulum and over Dick's brown rump, hardly brushing it at all.

"There now, I told you I could do it," she exclaimed with unconcealed satisfaction. "Take care, little dogies, here comes Hippity-Hoppity-Along Hyland."

Her mother hugged Amy with unwarranted warmth as she watched Blythe ride toward her post after her first lightly casual mention of her handicap. She was literally sitting on top of her world on Dick's back and after waiting around at the appointed spot for a while she tired of inaction.

"Maybe they're having trouble with the cattle. We'll ride to the top of the rise to see if we can see 'em, Dickie, my lad."

The pair ambled along pleasantly, admiring the scenery, stopping for a closer look at an ocotillo cactus in bloom, tiny red flowers scattered the length of long whiplike canes covered with metal-sharp thorns.

"Looks prettier alive than lined up across the front of the yard for a fence, doesn't it?"

Blythe was so absorbed in her nature study she was almost to the top of the little ridge that cut off her view when she became aware of a chorus of lowing and bawling accompanied by the sound of many hoofs and the yells of her father and brothers. She checked Dick sharply, her heart in her mouth.

Where to hide? She well knew that if the herd came over the hill and faced her point-blank the whole bunch might

scatter, but the sparse range growth there would hardly have
hidden a rabbit. There was only one thing to do and reckless though it seemed it was better than facing her father's
anger as his day's work scattered to the four winds.

With her left hand she wheeled the cow pony and her
right hand grasped the comforting horn as she kicked him
into a gallop. Her hat blew off and bounced about on her
back, held there by the chin strap. A jack rabbit popped up in
front of them and raced madly ahead, too startled to swing
away to one side, as Dick rocketed toward the corrals.

Sudden though their turn and start had been, Blythe kept
her head and her balance, rejoicing that her horse was so well
reined that a turn of the wrist corrected any feeling of inse-
curity. It was a short run but long enough for Blythe to glory
in her speed and the wind whipping past her face.

One part of her mind thrilled to the realization that it was
just as easy to ride a gallop as a canter while another part
wondered how she would ride out the sudden, jolting stop
common to stock horses. Hand and voice combined to cut
Dick's speed, once they were near their assigned post, and
they came around in a large circle on the left lead that slowed
him to a hand canter which was but a few steps from a halt.

The herd was only then spilling over the rise and Mr.
Hyland spotted Blythe in her place, as motionless as though
she had been waiting for hours. If he had had his binoculars
with him, Dick's rapid breathing and a disheveled, happy
look about his daughter would have been reminiscent of
nights he had looked into the children's room to make sure
they were asleep and had been greeted by an electric darkness
and feigned slumber.

Thenceforth Blythe paid stricter attention to her duties, and one by one the pastures were combed and each night a new bunch was added to the herd in the home pasture. She began to think that her father had manufactured her particular job just to make her feel that she was helping. His request at supper the night before their last day's gathering proved her wrong.

"Are you up to a little longer ride tomorrow, Blythe?"

"Sure I am, Dad. Where to and what for?"

"The first day when we brought in the cows from the south pasture there was one old girl who was too smart for us—"

"And wouldn't let you bring her in?"

"No, not just that. We found her at the first water hole and she'd hid out her calf some place. We waited a bit to see if she might lead us to him but she wouldn't do it so we left her as I figured we'd find him during the course of our riding, but we never did and I don't like to leave an unbranded calf. I thought maybe if you felt like it you could mosey up there and look around for them. Chances are that they'll be down at the water together by now."

"Think she'll let me bring her in all right?"

"Sure, she's probably a little lonesome by now. If she still has him hid, you might hang around and sooner or later she'll get nervous and head back to him and you just tag along at a respectful distance."

"Daddy," Amy pressed for attention. "What do you mean the mama had hidden her baby? How?"

"Well, sugar, it's this way. Most of the time when a bunch of cows and calves are a long way from water the cows find a likely thicket and take turns watching several calves while the other cows go to water. With several together they're easy to find, but sometimes one wise old girl likes solitude and when she's thirsty she just tells Mister Baby to lie down under a bush and not to move until she gets back. He won't either, unless we run right on to him and drive him out, and she's too smart to lead us back to him. It takes time and patience—more of both than I had the other day."

Blythe's chest measurements expanded several inches in as many minutes while her father gave her what pointers he could. She was all business the next morning when she rode off soon after the others.

It was a fairly short ride to the water hole but neither cow nor calf was in sight, so she headed for the draw where her father thought the calf had been, but careful riding back and forth brought no results. She debated whether to return to the water hole or go on riding the pasture in the hope of running across her quarry. The latter sounded like a pretty large program and she decided on another trip to the water.

The morning freshness was already giving way to a pleasant warmth that promised another hot day and Blythe hoped to complete her mission and be home before the blistering afternoon. She set Dick into the dry course of a creek since its bush-lined banks made it a favorite hide-out for cattle. Still no luck. When she calculated they were about opposite the water hole, Dick was turned and they scrambled up the side just as the cow ambled into view on the opposite side.

"Oh, shucks, Dick. I wish we'd been a minute later. Now she knows we're here and will get cagey. Well, we have just as much patience as she has—I hope!"

As the day wore along Blythe began to doubt her statement. The cow satisfied her thirst but then showed no disposition to return to her calf. Blythe let Dick have a few sips of water and then retreated to the shelter of the creek bed where she sat sidesaddle to rest her leg, peering out through the bushes at the cow that was too smart to think horse and rider had left for good.

Finally the breathless heat in the draw drove Blythe out into the open where a slight breeze made the temperature more bearable. She shifted around into many positions, vainly seeking one that would rest her as she looked wistfully at the inviting ground. Dreaming of the buckskin helped pass the time but as the hours dragged along even that diversion lost its magic and Blythe came to realize that she had two courses open to her, sticking it out in spite of her hunger and discomfort or returning empty-handed.

"By cracky, we'll stay here, old girl, if it takes all night," the girl decided, "but that means I'll have to get off for a while. You'd better co-operate when I'm ready to mount, Dickie, old boy, or we'll be sitting here when they come looking for us!"

Blythe calculated her chances carefully and rode Dick up by a pile of rocks which had been grubbed out of the water hole sometime when it was deepened. There she dismounted stiffly and stretched out gratefully on the ground. Comfort flowed through her like a tonic as her muscles relaxed, and she sighed blissfully. Dick's reins had been dropped over his head and the veteran cow pony was ground-tied as tightly as though he had been tethered to a stout tree. Half asleep, he stood patiently beside her, his head drooping, one hip sagging.

Blythe had just begun to enjoy the relief of her new position when Dick pricked up his ears and turned his head,
making her sit up. Exasperation boiled up within her at the
sight of the cow's red rump and ropey tail disappearing between the bushes that lined the trail.

"Drat that beast! If she isn't the contrariest critter on four
legs I've ever met. It's our move, Dick, and we'd better make
it fast or we'll lose the old girl yet."

Blythe leaned one hand on the horn and hopped over to
the rocks she had picked out for a mounting block. She turned
the horse's right side toward her and, placing her hands on
the cantle and pommel, she gave a little spring which threw
her weight onto her stiffened arms. Then it was her left leg
that she threw across the saddle with comparative ease.

"Didn't dare take any chances of not getting my game leg
across you this time. Come on, let's tag along."

She was vexed to discover how close the calf had been all
the time, for five minutes' riding brought them up with the
cow and her hungry calf. Blythe circled them and reined in
at a discreet distance to wait for the bumptious youngster to
satisfy his appetite; wondering just how cantankerous the
cow would be when she tried to drive her. As Blythe and
Dick closed in slowly it seemed as if the cow said "I give up"
and, followed by the calf, she turned and shambled down the
trail.

This time instead of the fast walk that so delighted his
rider, Dick adopted the little hesitation step that the true cow
pony uses when driving cattle. Blythe slouched comfortably
in the saddle and so it was that her father and Dan met them.

"We got worried when we found you weren't home yet. What happened?"

After Blythe's account of her day's work her father broke into a pleased smile.

"Good going, hon! That makes you one of our top hands for sure."

VI: The Hyland Cowboys

THE BRANDING IRONS were not yet hot the next morning before two mounted men were seen approaching. Such open country left no possibility of a surprise visit, for cars and horses were plainly visible long before arrival, so Mr. Hyland could notify his family that their nearest neighbor, "Also" Russell, was coming to call.

"Is his name really 'Also,' Pop?" Chris asked curiously.

"No, but I guess it's just as unusual. His name is Russell Russell, so, of course, everyone calls him 'Also.' Wonder what he has on his mind?"

"We're new here. Maybe he just wants to make sure we keep our branding iron where it belongs," Dan suggested.

"Well, if that's all, he could have saved himself a lot of effort. Come on, let's get moving. We don't want to look like a bunch of city slickers. Here's how we'll do it. Dan and I'll do the roping, flanking and tying. Chris can bring us the irons as we need them and handle the gate when we want animals in or out, and Blythe and Dick will do the driving."

"Me, Daddy, what about me?" Amy clamored.

"I'm coming to that. You can bring us the serum and needle and antiseptic."

"What about me, Daddy?" Mrs. Hyland pantomimed Amy's question.

"You can have a walloping big dinner ready for us when we come in. We'll need it and we'll be ready for it—but until time to start you can help Amy by filling the needle. Let's go. Which calf do you pick, Dan?"

"That one!"

Dan's rope circled once or twice and settled over a strapping calf that deafened them with its bawling when the loop drew tighter. Mr. Hyland ran in and threw it to the ground where, with a few quick motions, he tied its legs together. The other Hylands carried out their roles as though they had been rehearsed and it was not until Mr. Calf was up and scampering back to his mates that the Hyland cowboys realized their visitors had arrived.

The two men sat their horses just outside the corral and watched the proceedings approvingly. One was a wiry individual with a weather-marked face and shiny black eyes. From their advance billing everyone knew that the big, blue-eyed man in the felt sombrero was "Also" Russell and the small, dark man his foreman.

" 'Morning, Hyland. Heard in town yesterday that you'd be branding today so Luis and I rode over to see if we could help you out any. From the way you just handled that big fellow looks as though you've got a pretty able crew already."

"That's mighty nice of you, Mr. Russell." Tyler Hyland's eyes crinkled with friendliness at so neighborly a gesture. "There's no telling when we'll need replacements. Why don't you step down and tie your horses there in the shade while we see how things go. First of all, you'd better meet my hands."

Each member of the family was introduced to the visitors in turn. The four youngsters tried to appear glad to see their neighbor in spite of their jealous feelings that he might make their services unnecessary. Time resolved that problem, however, and as more and more calves joined the "finished" bunch each young worker welcomed the thought of relief. The work went along smoothly without any feeling of hurry and Mr. Hyland wisely took ample time for recesses.

Dinnertime found the group in fine spirits, conscious of a good morning's work and plenty of energy left for the remainder of the job. Working with the family as they had, the visitors soon felt like old friends, making it a merry tableful with many a laugh as they recalled highlights of their morning's work.

"Someday when you haven't anything to do—no, I don't mean that, I know ranch work is never finished—someday whether you have anything to do or not, Ty"—Blythe noted that Mr. Russell and her father had already gone on to given names—"I wish you'd bring your family over for a visit. I'm sure your young folks would be interested in my horses."

"They would indeed. They're all horse-crazy, except maybe Amy and her specialty is babies—whether it's chicks, kittens, calves or colts. Mr. Russell raises horses, kids, or I should say specifically palominos, and dandies."

"Is that all, Mr. Russell? Don't you have cattle too?" Dan couldn't understand a ranch without a bread-and-butter crop of beef, and how right he was was proved by their neighbor's answer.

"Oh, sure, more cattle really than horses. They're just a hobby with me. Luckily you have to have horses too if you're running cattle."

"Do you ever have trouble with rustlers, Mr. Russell?" Chris asked, wide-eyed. "You know with the border right here and—and everything."

"Life on a ranch isn't exciting enough for Chris. He's always trying to cook up some extra thrills," his father explained tolerantly.

"No, Chris, I can't say that we do—at least not lately."

"Then you did once? How many head did they take? How'd they do it?"

"Easy, lad, easy. I was going to say that about five years ago I did miss one of my best brood mares and her foal, a filly almost old enough to wean. They just disappeared into thin air, so it seemed they must have been stolen."

"Five years ago, hmm?" Mr. Hyland appeared to be doing mental arithmetic. "Was that by any chance that extra wet winter you had?"

It was Mr. Russell's turn to be thoughtful and he turned to Luis for help.

"Yes, come to think about it, it was. Why?"

"Did the filly happen to be a buckskin?"

Mr. Russell and Luis exchanged surprised glances and the former's voice betrayed his puzzlement.

"Yes, she was, but how do you happen to know so much about her?"

Mr. Hyland's reply was lost in the exuberant cries of his children.

"The buckskin! The lost buckskin! She didn't fly in after all!"

Only Blythe was silent, and tears choked her so she couldn't have spoken. She seized her crutches, rose so suddenly her chair toppled over backwards, and hobbled hurriedly from the room to hide the tears that threatened to overflow momentarily.

The startled visitors stared uncomprehendingly at their host who hastened to give an explanation of the tumult. When Blythe rejoined them a little later Mr. Russell's first remark seemed merely to carry on the same subject.

"If she hadn't been a buckskin, I might have been more upset, but a buckskin only reminds a palomino breeder of a failure. I would have liked to find her mother though I wasted few tears on her."

"She's a good-looking mare now though. You'd be proud of her. Breeding stands out all over her."

Blythe shot a resentful glance at her father. Why did he have to keep on singing the buckskin's praises?

"Oh, she has breeding all right. Half Morgan and half Arabian—but she's still a buckskin. No, Ty, you're welcome to her and you can keep her in your Pocket as long as you want to."

Mr. Russell twinkled a little as he grandly renounced all ownership.

"Suppose she weren't down in the bottom of the Pocket? Would that change your mind, Mr. Russell?"

Dan's tone was teasing, but Blythe sensed a more serious purpose behind his words. Her breathing deepened after their neighbor's reply.

"I don't think so, Dan. I don't want her and it'd only mean I'd have to get rid of her some other way. No, in the Pocket or out she's a Hyland now and if you can teach her to high jump out of there, you'll really have something. Ringling Brothers would give her top billing for her 'Hyland fling.'"

Blythe itched to talk to Dan alone. That question he had asked Mr. Russell meant something, she felt sure. It was not until mid-afternoon when she gave up her mounted job in favor of watching from the sidelines that she and Dan had a minute together. He came over and flopped down beside her during an intermission.

"What've you got up your sleeve, Dan?"

"Me? Just my arm. See." He extended a well-muscled brown arm on which the sunburned hairs made streaks of gold.

"Quit stalling. I'm sure you found out something at the Pocket that you haven't told. Give!"

"Maybe it's a false hope, Sis. I've been afraid to mention it for fear it'd get you all steamed up over nothing."

"I'm steaming now, so you might as well tell me. What'd you find when you rode off by yourself that day?"

"That brushy side canyon we had to detour seemed like the only possible place for a trail down into the Pocket and I rode back to snoop around."

"And is it?"

"Persistent, aren't you?"

"Is it?" Blythe's two words were less question than demand.

"Yes and no. I did find the start of an old trail, an old, old, old, *old* trail—but there must be a catch in it somewhere or the buckskin would have climbed out that way. So don't get your hopes up, Butch."

"I see what you mean. There must be an obstruction farther down—"

"Or else the trail peters out altogether, but before saying anything I thought we might as well get prior rights to the mare settled. Now she's all yours if we can get her."

"All mine! Why, Dan, why—why—"

"You wanted her, didn't you? You're improving so fast you'll soon outgrow old Dick. If you didn't want her, what'd you get so excited about her for?"

Dan was perplexed by his sister's silence and took it to mean that she wasn't really interested in the buckskin after all, while she was as dazzled as though a star had dropped in her lap. Heretofore it had all seemed like a fairy tale.

"Sure! Sure I want her," Blythe said faintly, "but I didn't think it'd ever mean anything more than that I owned the mare in the Pocket. But, Dan, she isn't even broken. How can I—how could I—"

"Sidetrack that worry for a while. We'll have plenty bigger ones before we get to that. Mum's the word yet."

Dan returned to the branding corral but it no longer held Blythe's attention. She was in the midst of a fairy tale come true. The buckskin would be her own magic carpet, her devoted slave. Blythe pictured herself flying over the ground, herself and her horse as one. So enthralled was she by her visions she hardly understood the meaning of her father's satisfied exclamation, "Good! That does it!"

"Now can we turn 'em all loose, Pop?" Chris asked as they herded the calves back into the big corral where their anxious mothers had stood staring and lowing uneasily throughout the day.

"Well, we could, but it's safer if we mother 'em out."

"What's that, Daddy?" Amy's ear caught the word "mother" and she was all attention.

"It's this way, punkin. After we've handled the calves and they smell of antiseptic and scorched hair, sometimes the cow isn't sure the calf is hers. If we turned 'em loose, most of 'em would get along all right but one or two disowned young ones might starve."

"But what can we do to help?"

"We just watch them here together and when we see a calf nursing, that means his mommy has accepted him and we shove them out the gate together, happy. Pairing them up a few at a time, there's hardly any that won't take their calves but if we just turned them out, calves might rush at the wrong cow and get butted and the noise and confusion would make them all wilder."

"Amy can have Dick if she wants to be in the corral with you, Dad," Blythe offered, loath to leave off her dreaming. "I'll bet she'll be able to sense which cow and calf go together from the look in their eyes."

Patience was about all it took and Blythe found it so interesting she was unable to get back into her dream. The riders sat motionless, watching the herd until they spotted a

happy pair which they eased through the throng to the gate
Chris quickly threw open.

Cries of "Here's a couple," "These are ready to go," or
perhaps one of the men's cautious advice to wait a bit to make
sure of a doubtful cow punctuated the calm that had settled
when the branding was finished. Once a smart old girl got
through by mistake and Luis on his nimble bay brought her
back. Amy proved herself worthy of her sister's confidence
and not one pair that she spotted was mismatched.

Mr. Russell and Luis prepared to leave despite their host's
urgent invitation to stay for supper before their long ride
home.

"Thanks just the same, Ty, but we'd better be going on or
Sarah'll send out a posse to look for us. But you know what
I'd like? Sometime when you're heading over toward the
Pocket, I'd like to go along with my telescope and see whether
I can see any sign of my brood mare there. You say you didn't
see anything of her?"

"Neither hide nor hair. It doesn't seem as if she's there or
the buckskin wouldn't act so terribly lonely, but by all means
come along. How about Saturday?"

Mr. Hyland was about to say the next morning but one
look at Blythe's eyes, blazing with eagerness but ringed with
blue smudges of fatigue, made him postpone the ride a few
days.

"When we go, you can ride on ahead with the boys and
Blythe and I will come along later in the pick-up. It's still a
little too far for her to ride."

"I've got a better plan, Ty. You ride on with the boys and

I'll come over with Golden Go in my two-horse trailer, load up Dick and squire Miss Hyland myself. How's that?"

"Couldn't be better. That'll mean the boys and I can check on the cattle as we go along and see how the branded calves are making it. See you Saturday, neighbor, and thanks a million for your help."

VII: Meant for Each Other

BLYTHE WAITED for Mr. Russell Saturday morning with mixed feelings. Every nerve crawled with impatience to get started for the Pocket, but the aversion for strangers she had felt since her illness sprang up unbidden and made her wish she did not have to ride with Mr. Russell. Only the beckoning buckskin prevented her from feigning a headache that would keep her at home.

She had liked him very much the day of the branding, but there had been others around to make her feel less conspicuous. Would she be able to get into his car without sprawling or dropping a crutch? What in the world could she think of to say? Surely they couldn't ride that far together in silence! Of course, there was always the weather but so even a climate hardly offered material for many minutes' conversation.

Blythe had herself worked up to such a pitch that she thumped into her room and closed the door when she saw car and trailer turn into the yard. She couldn't go! She heard the kitchen door open and a woman's birdlike chirping against the background of Mr. Russell's baritone.

"Hello, Mary Hyland, I'm Sarah Russell. I just told 'Also' I was coming along with him, that this would be a good chance for me to get acquainted with all of you. He's talked of nothing but the Hylands since he was over here and I felt cheated."

"I'm so glad you did. Here, let me put your hat in the girls' room."

Her mother's footsteps came toward the door and rather than be caught just standing there, Blythe opened the door and walked out. Mrs. Russell just matched her voice, being tiny and pert and always fluttering.

"This must be Blythe. I'm so glad to meet you. And here's Amy," the older woman exclaimed as Amy came in from the living room. "And you have two boys, too. That seems almost unfair when we haven't any children. 'Also' said he had half a notion to slap our brand on a couple of yours the other day so's we could claim them."

"Might have at that if you folks hadn't been watching me so close," he chuckled heartily.

"You two go on with you now. We womenfolk have too much to do to have you underfoot, haven't we, Amy?"

"Wait just a minute, Mrs. Russell, while I see whether they'll need any help getting Dick in the trailer. I don't know how easy he loads." Blythe's mother made a move toward the back door.

"You go on with your 'woman's work' Sarah's always

talking about and don't worry about us. We'll make out all right. Won't we, Blythe?"

His heartiness left no room for dispute though Blythe wondered how much good she'd be if Dick hung back at all, but he walked in like the veteran he was. While Mr. Russell was fastening the tail gate, Blythe opened the car door and scrambled in as quickly as she could so that she was all settled when he came to help her.

They waved to the stay-at-homes and headed for the east mountains. Blythe frantically cast about for some topic of conversation, but nothing offered itself.

"This country doesn't look like much, but it sure grows on you," Mr. Russell said, as much to himself as to her. "It must have been beautiful though when the old-timers first came through."

"Was it any different then than it is now?" Blythe asked in surprise.

"Oh, sure. The early ranchers overgrazed it so there's little left of the original grass. Why, they say there was grama grass waist-high then—so thick that a man with a jackknife could cut a night's feeding for his horse in no time at all. About the only grass to survive is the sacaton. That's good—what's left of it."

"Yes, the stock really seems to eat it up," Blythe agreed with a feeble attempt at a joke. "I suppose you feed real hay to your prize horses, don't you?"

"Sometimes yes, sometimes no, depends on the condition of the range. You're pretty fond of horses, aren't you? I can tell from the way you handle them."

"Oh, yes, I love 'em. We used to live on a ranch, you know,

until I was about Amy's age, and my ambition was to grow up and raise horses. But now—I don't know—" Her voice trailed off into silence.

"Why not? Haven't lost your ambition, have you?" he teased.

"We-e-ll, no, but it hardly seems practical now."

"But it's plenty of fun. Just wait until you see some of my honeys. That'll change your mind."

"Without seeing the rest, I can tell you that in my opinion you've given away the best horse you ever owned."

"Given away? What do you—? Oh, now I see. You mean the buckskin. Well, that's one of the good things about horses. No two people seem to like the same one. So she's your choice, with the others sight unseen?"

"Oh, yes, just wait until you see her. Such speed, such action, and she's so graceful and pretty. She's a beauty all right," Blythe exclaimed fervently.

Mr. Russell's eyes were thoughtful as he maneuvered the car and trailer over an unusually rough section of road before replying.

"Sounds as though she's your horse of horses all right. But worship from afar isn't much fun."

"No, but I can always hope for a miracle. She's worth one. Just you see."

Notwithstanding Blythe's superlatives, Mr. Russell was not prepared for the buckskin's picture of wild beauty when she rushed to the top of her lookout and neighed a welcome to the cavalcade on the rim. Since their first visit she had been uneasy and had spent much of her time pacing her prison rather than enjoying it for the perfect pasture it was.

"She's lost weight," Blythe cried in alarm. "I hope she isn't sick."

"No horse with the sheen to its coat that she has is sick," her father pointed out matter-of-factly. "Well, what d'ya think of her, 'Also'?"

The latter's telescope had been pinpointed on the mare for some minutes as he admired in silence. A long whistle was his only comment but Blythe understood that he completely agreed with her. Putting two fingers to her mouth she split the air with a two-note whistle of admiration. The mare tossed her head nervously, the silken strands of her foretop and mane tumbling about her ears and eyes.

"Why, Butch, I thought you'd forgotten how to whistle on your fingers." Dan was more taken with his sister's accomplishments for the moment than he was with the mare. "Do it again."

Blythe obliged and this time the mare spun on her haunches and dashed to another vantage point where she answered with a whinny. Her forefoot struck out and she pawed violently.

"Hey, Bucky, come on up here." Chris had not yet learned the advanced whistle so he substituted a lusty bellow. Blythe whirled on him.

"Don't you call her Bucky. That's not her name."

"All right, Miss Brains. I suppose you know of a better one?"

"You bet I do. Her name from now on is Dark Sunshine."

"Dark Sunshine, eh? Sa-ay, not bad," the boy agreed. "I suppose it's Darky for short then?"

"No, goon, if you can't go on to the next syllable, I'll help you. It's Sunny for short."

"Hey, Butch, that's all right," Dan said admiringly. "When'd you dream that one up?"

"The other night when I couldn't get to sleep. The name just popped out at me. It was almost as if someone said it out loud."

"Probably you did, hon, but take it easy. You've got a horse and a name and all that's standing between you is thin air—but what a lot of it," her father said warningly. "Don't set your heart on the unattainable. It's a bad habit to get into. Make you a lot of trouble before you're as old as I am."

Blythe and Dan exchanged glances, asking each other if this was the time to tell their secret, yet they hesitated by tacit agreement. Mr. Russell had not said a word since he first saw the mare though his telescope had been trained on the Pocket all the time.

"I don't see a sign of her mother. Guess she lost out somehow. Blythe, that's a wonderful name for a wonderful mare and if I had any magic spell, I'd certainly get her out for you—but I'm afraid the age of miracles is past."

Mr. Russell shook his head forlornly and went back to admiring Dark Sunshine. There was agreement in Dan's and Blythe's glance that time.

"Maybe not, sir. It's just possible we *might* be able to get her out of there."

His father and Chris and Mr. Russell stared at Dan in amazement, almost as if they expected to see him shake out a magic carpet. Mr. Hyland's expression soon changed to anger.

"Don't lead her on like that, Dan! You'll only build her hopes up to heartbreak if you do."

"I'm not so sure, Dad." Dan stood up to his father with a steadiness that was not to be shaken. "When we were here before I rode down into that brushy gulch a ways and found an old, old trail—probably an Indian trail. Maybe there wasn't always just the gateway that was closed. This might even have been a game trail—but anyway, it may be a way out for the buc—I mean Dark Sunshine."

"It can't be passable now or she'd have used it."

"I know, that's what I told Blythe, but don't you think it's worth investigating? Whatever is in the way might not be too much for us to move even if a horse couldn't."

"I suppose it won't hurt to find out. Let's have a look."

They turned and circled the Pocket until they came to the ravine and Dan told them to halt. Everyone, including Blythe, dismounted and she was made comfortable on a blanket before the men turned to follow Dan, Mr. Russell as eager as any boy playing "explorer." Chris was about to fall in line until his father decreed otherwise.

"You stay to look after the horses and to keep Blythe company—and just in case we aren't back within three, four hours at the outside, you'd better go and get some reinforcements."

"Where from, Pop?" Chris looked helplessly at the lonesome miles around them.

"Back down to the road, turn east and after a while you'll get to Williams's place. This's really his land we're on, you know. Don't get yourself worked up to a hero's stature though. I don't expect it will be necessary."

Her father's tone was light but suddenly Blythe realized what they were attempting, to satisfy her girlish whim. She almost called them back, but that would have made her feel even sillier. After all they were grown men and able to look out for themselves.

"We might just take our ropes along. Probably won't need 'em but they might come in handy and we sure won't want to have to come back up for them," Mr. Hyland suggested, untying his from his saddle. The others followed his example.

The trio disappeared in the thickets and for a few minutes Blythe could trace their progress by their voices but they too faded away and she and Chris were faced with the hardest job of all, waiting. One hour passed. The second hour trailed by listlessly. The third hour was unbearably slow, made more so by Chris who had tired of his short trips of exploration and returned to stud the silence with lugubrious comments.

"I'm hungry. Let's eat our lunches." He made his first matter-of-fact statement in a long time.

"I'd rather wait and eat with the others when they come back."

"I wouldn't. I'm going to eat now. After all, I may have to be in trim for a long, hard ride for help."

"Oh, stop it!" Blythe cried furiously. "Quit trying to make yourself so dramatic. And it wouldn't be polite to eat before our guest does."

"I'm hungry now," Chris countered relentlessly.

"All right, eat then!"

For a time the silence was broken only by her small brother's exaggerated enjoyment of his food but the papers were soon crumpled and stowed back in the bag. Blythe's stomach was pinched but whether from hunger or anxiety she couldn't tell. She began to wonder uneasily how long they should wait before Chris rode for help. Each minute she told herself she would suggest it in a little while.

A faint, far whistle ended her suspense. It was Dan's signal. They were all right! Chris rushed down the trail like a welcoming terrier to meet them. The waiting girl had only to look at their expressions to know that they had met with some measure of success.

"Whew! Cowboy boots sure weren't meant for mountain climbing," Dan panted as he threw himself to the ground. The older men hadn't wind enough for that much talk for the moment.

"You sound like a wind-broken nag," Blythe giggled with relief. "You three take it easy and Chris and I will set out the eats for you."

The latter was a little sly fun at Chris's expense, for she well knew that had there been food enough his small-boy appetite would make it easy for him to eat again. She hastily opened saddlebags and spread out sandwich packets, content to wait for details.

"It really looks, Blythe, as though you and Sunny were meant for each other," was her father's first comment.

"Then the trail is all right?"

"It's no four-lane highway but what there is is good—seems to have been actually chipped out of solid rock by Indians maybe centuries ago."

"The Pocket was probably a favorite camp site for them but in case of attack by another tribe on the warpath they wanted to make sure of a back exit," Mr. Russell added, "and they made it big enough to bring all their possessions along."

"It looks a lot better once you're on it than you'd think from the top, but there is a landslide across the trail clear down at the bottom, Sis, only fifty or a hundred feet from where it opens out onto the floor of the Pocket."

"Oh-h," she exhaled with disappointment. "I thought there'd be a catch in it. These mountains must be pretty uneasy for all that they look so solid."

"It's not a bad one. Doesn't cover more than ten or fifteen feet of the trail. Two or three days' work ought to clear it enough to get a horse across."

"Were you able to get over it? That must have been dangerous!"

"Yes and no. We tied ourselves together and inched across one at a time."

Blythe thought that over in silence until the full import of what her father said came to her.

"Then you've been down in the Pocket! What'd it seem like?"

"Like a long way back," Dan answered for all of them, "but it showed us it can be done. Now all we have to figure out are the details."

CHARLES BOGGS
&
HANGED MAY 8TH
1869
&
"BY MISTAKE"
SORRY

VIII: Back Stairway

BLYTHE HAD been almost incoherent with happiness at knowing that the lost buckskin wasn't lost forever, and Mr.
Hyland was peppered with "when's" and "how's" until he
was dizzy. He finally took refuge from his children's per-
sistence in the statement that he couldn't make any definite
plans before talking it over with their mother.

Mr. Russell and Blythe made a gentlemen's agreement not
to break the good news to the home folks until the others
were there too. This seemed only fair, in view of their share
in the day's success, and also politic, inasmuch as Mr. Hyland's was the deciding vote. The riders had been given a
good start and then the car followed very slowly.

The impatient girl had expected the ride home to be endless but Mr. Russell picked up the thread of their conversation where it had been dropped that morning and Blythe, who no longer thought of him as a stranger but an old friend, easily followed his conversational paths.

"You like to read, don't you, Blythe?" At her nod he continued. "My hobby, one of them anyway, is collecting accounts of early days in this section and I have several that I'm sure would be fascinating reading for you. Come over some day and we'll go through them. One, for instance, tells how the town of Tombstone came to be founded and named."

"That's where Boothill Cemetery is, isn't it?"

"Yes, and you'll read almost as much history of this country's wild, rough days on those markers as in any book. There's one ironic epitaph for a man who was 'hanged by mistake.' Most of the rogues deserved what they got, however."

"Was it your father or grandfather who first settled here—not that I mean there's any connection between them and the rogues," she explained in sudden embarrassment at her blunder.

His throaty laugh proved he held no grudge and she was soon laughing too.

"It was Grandfather Russell, Blythe, who came out here to settle in the days when 'scalping' didn't mean selling tickets at exorbitant prices. Dad used to raise my hair for me with some of the tales Granddad told him. It's all right with me that those 'good old days' *are* gone forever!"

One topic led to another and they were back at the Lazy SL before it seemed possible. Dick was unloaded by the corrals and unsaddled and, with Blythe's coaching, Mr. Russell stowed away the tack in the right place. This delaying action enabled the riders to come in and care for their mounts before they all trooped up to the house.

"Land sakes, you folks back already?" Mrs. Russell cried in surprise. "Didn't expect to see you for hours."

"We've been down at the barn for some time, Sarah, or didn't you stop talking long enough to use your eyes," her husband scolded playfully.

"Well, how's the miracle buckskin today?" Mrs. Hyland asked her daughter.

"Careful, Mary, careful. Don't ever call her the buckskin again. She has a name now, Dark Sunshine," her husband warned.

"And that ain't all, Ma. She's got a back stairway!" Chris exploded their good news in one sentence.

Everyone talked then and the ladies had to be quick to piece out the story from the rapid-fire conversation. Mrs. Hyland grew more and more thoughtful, Blythe also, for she knew what her mother was thinking.

Would it be wise? Blythe dreaming about a beautiful buckskin was one thing but having her was something else again.

The girl's hands clenched into fists and every muscle tensed. She was momentarily diverted to note that even the tendons in her right leg were tight, but they relaxed suddenly at her mother's resigned words.

"Well, I suppose there's no use thinking any ranch work will get done so long as Dark Sunshine is unredeemed."

"It's not quite that bad, Mary. With the branding out of the way there's kind of a lull now—just routine stuff that can be done any time."

"How'll you go about it, Ty?"

"About the only way there is, I guess, Mary. Dan and I'll pack over and camp down in the Pocket while we're clearing the trail."

"Then what? Maybe the mare doesn't understand as well as we seem to what her destiny is."

"Dad, can't I go too?" Blythe's whole heart was in her eyes. "I won't be in the way. I'll even be able to do the cooking for you. Can't I, Dad?"

Mr. Hyland's mouth opened to veto her suggestion, to say that it was no place for a lame girl, and he nearly choked to bite back the words.

"How're you going to get down there, hon?" he managed instead.

"Well-l, I'll walk!" she said stoutly.

"Dad, if the trail's to be good enough to bring a horse up, it ought to be all right for one to go down," Dan reasoned. "Why can't I lead Dick down to the slide? We can soon fix that enough so Blythe can creep across and I can help her down the rest of the way."

"Where does that leave Dick?" his mother put in.

"Turn him loose and he'll go back up by himself to where we've hobbled our horses. He'll stick around with them."

"Say, Ty, I've got some dynamite over home if that'd help you any," Mr. Russell offered.

"It sure would, 'Also,' but I'm afraid to use it. Suppose it touched off a larger slide? I'm sure none of us is angelic enough to sprout wings, and pretty as the Pocket is, I'd get pretty bored with a lifetime of it!"

"I can go too, can't I, Pop?" Chris began to be worried at

not hearing his name mentioned and hastened to put in his bid.

"No, son, you'll have to stay home and be the man of the house. Your mother will need your help—and we'll need your horse for a pack animal."

"To think that Blind Man's Pocket isn't so blind after all," Mrs. Hyland marveled.

"Maybe I'll find I'm not so lame too," Blythe said with a casual gaiety that proved the expedition's worth.

The Lazy SL hummed with preparations and when the Hylands returned from town with supplies for the trip, Blythe went into such a frenzy of anticipation each minute was a lifetime. She hovered over their growing pile of duffle like an old hen.

"Don't touch anything, Amy, or we might find ourselves in the Pocket without something important," she warned. "Chris! That candy's not for you. It's quick energy while we're out," she explained with a big-sisterly air.

The morning they were to start Blythe was awake before even her mother was stirring, yet the girl lay abed, savoring her anticipated miracle. She was taking the first real step toward making Dark Sunshine her own. This thought loosed so many electric currents through her body and mind that lying still was hopeless. She crept out quietly and dressed in her "going away" clothes without waking Amy.

Mrs. Hyland, Chris and Amy took Blythe as far as they could in the pick-up where she changed to Dick for one-horse power travel. Just before the little pack train dipped out of sight in a dry wash, Blythe turned and waved to the stay-at-home Hylands who stood watching by the truck.

Then she set her face eagerly toward her Dark Sunshine in Blind Man's Pocket.

Neither her father nor Dan felt any more like talking than Blythe and they rode in comparative silence until reaching the rim where they paused for a quick peek into the Pocket. As though she had been waiting for them, Dark Sunshine popped into sight and cantered up to her lookout. Blythe's whistle cut the air and like an echo a shrill neigh followed.

"Almost sounds as if she's answering you, Sis. Try it again."

Again Blythe's signal spanned the distance from rim to floor. The buckskin's reply was less immediate but when the silence closed in over the whistle the mare sent back a questioning whinny. Mr. Hyland started to follow around the Pocket and just before going out of sight Blythe sent a third call back to the mare.

Thinking of the ordeal ahead soon eclipsed what attention Blythe would have given the buckskin when their trail permitted quick glimpses into the Pocket. It was not the motion of her horse, Blythe realized, that made her stomach seem to turn over in every direction.

Mr. Hyland looked around with a practiced eye once they arrived at the top of the trail. A small grove of stunted mesquites around a water hole would afford the hobbled horses feed and water and some protection from the sun. There they unsaddled.

"What in the name of common sense is this big sheet of tin you tied into the pack for, Dan? Did you think the load wasn't big enough and needed a little ballast maybe?"

"It's this way, Dad. That looked like a long way down to be pack horses ourselves and I figured that with gravity on our side we could stow our stuff on the tin and just slide downhill with it sort of. Good idea, huh?"

"Hrmph! A good idea if it works maybe. Suppose it gets away from us?"

"It won't. You can hold it from the front and I'll keep a rope on behind to steady it at the same time I'm leading Dick."

"Jiminy, Dan, are you the brain!" Blythe exclaimed admiringly, impressed anew at his resourcefulness.

"Well, come on, Einstein, and let's get the pack loaded on your toboggan. That's the only way to find out if it works," Mr. Hyland said with a grin.

In a remarkably short time everything was rearranged and the party was ready to start down. Blythe's expression was such a composite of expectancy and apprehension that Dan burst out laughing.

"Cheer up, Sis. It isn't as bad as you expect, but I will say that after this one the Grand Canyon Trail ought to be a cinch for you. All set, Dad, mush!" he called as if to a lead dog.

Dick pricked up his ears and snorted at the noise made by the metal-shod pack as it slid along the ground in front of him. A forefoot struck out tentatively.

"He looks like a kitten batting at a ball of yarn," Blythe chuckled. "Easy, boy, there's nothing to it. Don't get your dander up now, for goodness' sakes!"

Wise old horse that he was, he accepted either her reassurance or his own common-sense appraisal of the thing that seemed to keep going away from him, and settled down to extra careful progress. For a little way the trail wound through the scrub growth at the lip of the canyon only to dip down sharply at the first turn.

In spite of being merely a passenger, her safety entrusted to Dan and Dick, Blythe watched the trail like a hawk. Steep though it was the footing seemed good and Dick chose his way with the care that age learns, so that a foot was not picked up until he knew just where he intended setting it down. Once in spite of his care a back hoof slid forward suddenly but Dick collected himself cautiously without any of the nervous prancing of a younger horse.

The party was well down the trail before Blythe dared spare a look at her surroundings. The midday sun was filtered by the growth above, and the eerie twilight that deepened with each foot downward made them feel they were in another world from that of sun-drenched prairie.

The ravine sloped sharply until it became a sort of chimney down which the trail wound back and forth like a half-spiral staircase but, steep though it was, Blythe could tell that the trail had been built with infinite care. As her father had said, much of it seemed to have been chipped out of the rock wall itself and the pathway was almost entirely solid rock except for spots where sand and dirt had been washed across it during rains.

Mr. Hyland halted occasionally for a rest when they struck an almost-level space and several times he and Dan pulled their shovels from the pack sled in order to improve the trail. Once during such a pause Blythe whistled but it seemed such an alien sound shrieking back and forth between the rock walls that she tried it no more. She had lost all track of time and felt that she and her father and Dan were floating be-

tween the now of being on the trail and the then when count-
less red men and women had built it.

Blythe began to peer ahead, thinking that it was time to
reach the slide but Dan, noticing her eagerness, warned her.

"Not for quite a while yet, Butch. Getting tired?"

"A little maybe, but mostly just curious."

She tried to occupy her thoughts with Dark Sunshine but
for once her dream horse could not hold her attention. Every
step each of them took was too vital for any wool-gathering.
To prove it the toboggan hit a slippery piece of sand and skittered toward the precipice. Blythe yelled a warning and the
men hauled in on their lines which stopped its forward, but
not its sidewise, progress.

Dan dropped Dick's lead line and dived for the sled which
he caught when one corner hung out into space. He lay in
the sand, panting with excitement for a minute before pulling their precious cargo back to safety and the right course.

"Whew! We'd have all this to do over again if we'd lost
our duffle. Not good. Not a bit good!"

Dick had frozen where he stood and was unwilling to take
another step until Dan retrieved the rein and patted his neck
comfortingly. Then the veteran consented to move forward.
After that Blythe really concentrated on their path so intently they were almost to the slide before she was aware of
it. She looked thoughtfully at the pile of rocks and rubble
that so completely filled the trail there was no ledge at all,
only the straight shoulder line from the mountain above to
the mountain below.

"That's a pretty imposing pile of stuff to be reckoned with.
It's a good thing I didn't know just how big it is or I mightn't
have been so urgent about getting Dark Sunshine out."

"That's what you say now we're too far to turn back," Dan joked. "Anyway, here's where you change trains. Need any help?"

Blythe made herself comfortable on the ground, her back to the reassuring wall. Dick was no daredevil and he too pressed close to the rock wall and stood motionless. The chestnuts on his legs, those horny calluses that every horse has, stood out like big warts. Blythe was reminded of a bit of folklore she had heard or read—that Indians rubbed their hands with chestnut flakes to help gentle their ponies. Eyes dancing, Blythe reached over and broke off several flakes which she stowed carefully in a pocket.

Meanwhile Mr. Hyland and Dan had attacked the slide with shovel and pickax. The girl could hear the dirt and rocks cascade into the bottom and when one extra big boulder was pried loose and rocketed down below they heard a series of terrified neighs from the Pocket.

"She remembers that old landslide too well. Bet it scared her to death," Mr. Hyland remarked.

When the men had leveled a little path over the rubble, Mr. Hyland prepared to cross the tricky section. First he took his rope and slipped one end over Dick's saddle horn and knotted the other around his chest under his armpits. Blythe and Dan understood the wisdom of this, for if he should slip over the edge they knew that the two of them never would be strong enough to pull him to safety.

Dropping on all fours he cautiously began to crawl up the steep slope of the slide. A loosened pebble rolled down, starting a small slide that gathered speed and size as it went, and Mr. Hyland fell flat until it ceased. He waited a minute, then resumed his creeping, and soon dipped over the crest and out of sight. The rope slithered along after him, taking up all the slack before it sailed back toward them.

"I'm across OK, kids. Now Blythe."

Her heart pounded out a double time as she slipped the rope over her shoulders and dropped on hands and knees. She wondered idly whether her father had deliberately crawled across since he knew she must. The rocks and dirt hurt her knees through her jeans though she hardly noticed the discomfort amid her larger worries, but her passage was completed without incident.

The pack sled was unloaded since it would surely have slipped off the uneven slide and one by one its contents were carefully eased over the crest and pushed down within Mr. Hyland's reach. Dan's final move before inching across with the empty toboggan was to remove Dick's saddle and bridle and leave him to make his way back to the horses above.

Blythe looked down the long trail to the Pocket and privately wondered how she would ever make it. Her father and Dan were reloading the sled, so she took her crutches and essayed a few steps.

"Well, I *can* do it—but it won't be easy," she muttered to herself.

"Come on, Sis. All aboard for Blind Man's Pocket. Climb on top of the duffle there," Dan explained when she only stared at him.

"I'm in your hands," she shrugged and, seating herself atop their pack, she rode down into the Pocket like Cleopatra on her barge.

IX: Love Potion

NEITHER Cortez nor Coronado nor De Soto was ever more charmed with a new vista than Blythe was on first viewing the Pocket from its own level. The ribbon of sparkling water gurgled along but a few yards from them and beyond was the open meadow rising to the little hill that was Dark Sunshine's lookout.

"What's our first and most important job, kids?"

"Throw a gate across that trail so Sunny won't slip away from us after all our toil," Blythe answered with unerring instinct.

"Right! Seeing tracks across that slide might lead her to try it—and that would be disastrous, if not fatal. I expected you to say make camp and get something to eat."

"That won't be amiss when the time comes," Dan agreed with a doleful look.

"Maybe we can be doing the two at once," Blythe suggested. "Let's pick out our camp site, Dad, and while you and Dan are building the gateway I can be unpacking our things and getting us squared away. What about that place? It's close."

She pointed to a sandy flat near the stream that was shaded by a couple of cottonwoods whose quivering leaves promised a pleasant breeze.

"Looks like 'home sweet home' to me," Dan agreed, and at his father's nod Dan dragged the sled to the spot. "I'd like steak and mushrooms with French fries, Butch, in case you get around to starting supper before we quit."

"That you shall have, Danny boy, but just for a lark I'm going to call it pancakes and bacon," his sister teased.

Blythe watched them return to the back stairway where they were lost to sight, but the ring of axes on wood guaranteed that there was no loafing. Taking the hint, she undid their bedrolls and spread them around where she thought the ground was the softest and unpacked their kitchenware and supplies. Long after she thought they had cut poles enough for seventeen gates, she could hear the two axes working, so the girl gladly turned her attention to Dark Sunshine.

Ears elert, the mare stood watching from a very respectful distance. She showed no signs of fear and her overabundance of curiosity, strong as any rope, held her near.

For the first time Blythe was able to see her good points at closer range and she could find no fault with her conformation. A small, intelligent head that showed its Arabian ancestry was set proudly on a delicate neck. Her well-formed withers crowned a sloping shoulder line that promised easy riding, while a short back and well-muscled, rounded rump spelled power and drive. All this perfection of form was mounted on four slender legs that tapered into nicely sloping pasterns and four dainty black hoofs that looked as polished and hard as flint.

Notwithstanding the mare's perfect build Blythe felt a small prick of disappointment. The close-up seemed so much duller and less wonderful than the distant vision. Like a child that catches at a beautiful soap bubble only to have its colors dissolve in a shower of soapy water, Blythe wanted to strike out at something and she kicked a shower of gravel with her toe.

Dark Sunshine wheeled on her haunches and raced away. Then Blythe's dream came true. The sun caught the buckskin's coat as it would a burnished shield and every hair reflected a golden glory. Her black legs glistened like new rubber boots—hip boots—for they extended halfway up the forearm and gaskin and stopped with a sharp line between the black and gold.

"I guess it's all done with mirrors, eh, Sunny?"

Blythe laughed at the mare's mincing progress back toward her, drawn again by her all-powerful curiosity. The girl repeated her whistle of admiration and was delighted to hear the mare's nostrils fluting a question.

The sound of axes had ceased and, making each move deliberately, Blythe picked up her crutches to return to her KP duty. For each step that she retreated the mare advanced one until she reached an imaginary line beyond which she would not go, contenting herself by watching the girl from a safe distance.

"You're snoopy, that's what you are, peering at your neighbors in such a bold, brazen way. Didn't your mommy teach you any better manners?"

Much as she would have liked to go on talking to Dark Sunshine, Blythe knew that the others would be ravenous and she hustled to be ready for them. So successful was she, they were greeted by the smells and sounds of boiling coffee and frying bacon.

"How come, Sis?" Dan held up Blythe's second crutch that lay beside their pile of duffle.

"Oh, it got in my way while I was cooking supper and I found I could get around pretty well without it. Well, wash up and rest a minute. Everything's ready but the pancakes and I didn't want to cook them until you were here and drooling for them," she said in high spirits.

"I am."

"Me too, if that's all the 'go ahead' you need!"

Their simple housekeeping caused little delay between supper and crawling into their beds, and they stretched out with happy sighs. Blythe looked up at the sky where the first stars were only then appearing and she could not have improved on the world at that moment.

"This's wonderful. I don't think I've had any nicer day than today since—since—" her illness seemed too far away and trivial to be worth mentioning—"since I was born, I guess. I hope you two feel the same." She yawned and stretched blissfully.

"It's tops with me," Dan agreed sleepily.

"Me, too, hon. 'S far as I'm concerned, it's well worth it," her father added, but Blythe fell asleep right in the middle of wondering what was worth what.

The next morning it was her turn to smell bacon and flap-jacks and to her surprise her father and Dan were already up, the former bending over their campfire, the latter teetering on a rock by the stream while he washed up with much splashing and spluttering. Blythe propped her head on an elbow and watched her father happily.

"Say, Dad, I was too sleepy to ask you last night. Why'd you cut so many poles? Seems like you must have enough there to build a house."

"It's this way, Blythe. We can't hang around here long enough to gentle that mare by easy stages, and so I decided we'd better build a corral. She isn't too wily but we can drive her in where I can rope and halter her. Then in that smaller area you can make up to her easier while we're building trail. You can't chase her all over the Pocket."

"It'll take a lot of work to build a corral high enough and stout enough to hold her."

"Yes, but it'll be faster and surer in the long run. I know how you feel, hon, and I'll be as gentle as I can, but we just don't have all summer."

Blythe stared into the fire, her mind in a turmoil, yet she knew that her father was right. After all, he and Dan were doing some back-breaking work to please her. She would have to play it their way.

"That's all right, Dad. I know you'll be careful—and we don't even have all month."

"All right. You'd better get up, skeeter, or you'll be late for breakfast."

"No breakfast in bed in this caravansary? What kind of a joint did we pick out for ourselves?" she complained jokingly while pulling on her boots and sweater, the only formality to dressing. "Smells like they have a good cook though. Ummm!"

Mr. Hyland went straight to work on the corral, having picked a spot where the cliffs receded into a deep bay and a fringe of trees around the mouth offered themselves as fence posts. Dan went back up the trail to retrieve the shovels they had left by the slide where they had expected to use them next. Blythe hastily cleaned up their camp before going over to lend her father what aid she could.

Just as she reached the corral site Dan returned from his trip up the trail, his expression a mixture of annoyance and surprise.

"What d'ya think? Old Dick was too scared to go back by himself and is right there where we left him last night, nickering his heart out for something to eat."

"That's a fine thing. It's lucky horses can sleep on their feet, but he'll get pretty hungry and thirsty before we're ready to leave," Mr. Hyland said with a short laugh, more annoyed than Dan.

"I can cut a little grass for him, Dad, to kind of keep him going. Seems like the least I can do for the old boy when he has helped me so much," Blythe offered.

"Let's work at clearing the trail first, Dad," Dan suggested, "so we can get him down here. Having him in the corral as a decoy might do a lot in gentling Dark Sunshine. What d'ya say?"

"Suppose we'll have to. Can't have him starving up there—but he certainly has thrown a monkey wrench into our work schedule."

Blythe took out her jackknife and began the laborious chore of cutting some of the tall, dry grasses the mare had left. The girl cut until a blister began to puff up on her finger but she had the satisfaction of seeing the little haycocks grow to a size that would provide Dick with an adequate meal when her father piled them into a blanket to carry up the trail.

"Just give a good yell if you want us for anything, Blythe," he advised as he and Dan turned toward the slide once more.

Blythe was secretly pleased that Dick had changed their plans since it gave her more time to court her buckskin mare. The evening before the mare had left as soon as the two men returned to camp. Mr. Hyland had heard her moving around near them during the night but Blythe had been unable to spot her all morning.

The girl returned to the place she had been the day before and scanned the valley floor but she saw no horse. Fingers and lips sent out her whistle that seemed to float endlessly on the still air. Again she called and strained her ears to listen. There! She heard scattering pebbles around the bend of the stream above camp and Dark Sunshine minced into view. She seemed to peer around cautiously as if to see whether she and Blythe were alone before continuing her forward progress.

Blythe hurriedly dug into a pocket and pulled out the pieces of Dick's chestnut she had secreted the day before. Choosing the softest, she rubbed it between her palms and over the backs of her hands until she herself could smell it. She cast an experienced glance at the waving leaves and grass.

"Lucky the wind's with me, Sunny. Now let's see how it works. Do I smell irresistible?"

The mare was undecided at first. She stopped in her tracks. Her neck stretched up wind as she sampled the tantalizing odor. She took a few more steps and her deep breaths distended her nostrils.

"Keep coming, girlie, it's for your own good if you only knew it. The friendlier you are now, the easier it'll be later."

Blythe's voice was a love song as she talked to the mare, her words frequently interspersed with their whistle—the one that Blythe hoped would become theirs. Many feet still separated the two but she was encouraged by the friendly look in the brown eyes that watched her so intently.

The girl rattled on and on, talking both sense and nonsense, to the mare who was, she knew, starved for company. Tiring at last of making conversation for the two of them, Blythe lapsed into song and discovered that Dark Sunshine had an ear for music. The girl crooned song after song with frequent returns to the *Indian Love Call*, as its words seemed most appropriate, while the mare listened contentedly. From time to time she took a few steps toward the girl who could hardly sing for wondering how close her horse would approach.

"At least you've never been mistreated by anyone so I don't have to overcome anything more than just your natural caution, Sunny," Blythe told her. "You've never known the human animal enough to have learned fear. I think we'll get along all right."

The sun was high and hot, reminding Blythe of her cooking duties. She slowly reached for her crutch which lay on the ground beside her and though it put the mare on her mark she made no move to leave until Blythe pulled herself erect. At that Dark Sunshine danced away a few steps.

"Come on, girl. Want to go and help get lunch?"

The buckskin did elect to tag behind at a safe distance, taking one step to Blythe's two. The latter was elated to see the mare cross the boundary where she had halted the evening before, not pausing until she hovered on the outskirts of camp. There she stopped and watched with interest while Blythe rekindled the fire and set the coffee pot on to boil. The first glimpse of the returning men sent her off to refuge in a thicket.

"Looks like you're making quite a little progress with your horse," her father commented. "It's too bad we'll have to rough her up when she's acting so docile."

"Yes, she doesn't seem to be a bit afraid of me, just cautious —but curious too. I think that once we get her in the corral and you're going to rope her, I'll get out of sight so she won't think I've had anything to do with it. Then maybe she'll let me come up to her sooner. Yes?"

"Yes, good idea. It won't be for a while though. It'll take us the rest of the day to get the trail so even old Dick can get across and we'll still have to build the corral and improve the trail a lot more before we'll dare take her across."

The minute the blue-jean-clad figures left camp Blythe whistled to Dark Sunshine who promptly popped out of her covert, whereupon the girl again picked up the strains of

"When I'm calling you-u-u-u-u-u." Since she had washed up before getting lunch, Blythe again rubbed her hands thoroughly with essence of chestnut while she hobbled slowly toward the mare. At any signs of restlessness Blythe halted until her singing had lulled the mare's fears, and then the snail-like forward progress was resumed.

As she had expected to sooner or later, she reached the place where her singing could no longer pacify the horse's uneasiness. There Blythe halted, leaning on her crutch, her other arm extended proffering a handful of grain. Its delightful fragrance filled Dark Sunshine's nostrils and made her mouth slaver with desire.

"Just a few more steps and it's yours, Sunny. Come on and make up with me. I wouldn't hurt you—not one little bit."

The mare took a step or two toward her and Blythe thrilled at their seeming nearness. She reached for her pocket with infinite caution and withdrew a lump of sugar. Its odor was so subtle the horse paid it scant attention until Blythe balanced it on her index finger and with a minimum of motion flipped it as she had many a marble.

The white square arced through the air and hit the ground just in front of Dark Sunshine who jerked her head in surprise but not alarm since the girl had scarcely moved. The black mane fell forward as the golden head and neck dipped to investigate. Dainty lips found the lump on the ground and pushed it about curiously while her nose urged more active appreciation. She picked it up and rolled it in her mouth, and as it dissolved the whole wonder of it reached her. Strong teeth crunched up the lump and the mare's head bobbed up and down in delighted surprise. When it was gone she looked to Blythe for more.

"Ah-ha, my proud beauty, you're as good as mine! You've eaten my love potion, a lump of sugar. It's just a matter of how and when!" Blythe crowed with restrained exuberance.

X: Sunny Day

No one was happier than Dick that evening when he was led down into the Pocket after his imprisonment in the dark, uncomfortable canyon. He spared scant attention for the beauties of his surroundings and dropped his head and began to graze greedily where he was hobbled.

Mr. Hyland and Dan returned to work on the corral when supper was finished and Blythe too was drafted to help hold poles in place. They worked furiously as long as there was daylight. Just when they felt they must stop, a bright moon graciously sailed up over the rim until at last only the gate was unfinished and they could do no more without daylight.

"Tomorrow morning we'll finish it up and get the mare in here—if we can—before Dan and I fix up the trail enough to take her across. That'll leave you a little time to work your charms on her, Blythe, to see what you can do," her father said wearily. "We might hobble Dick in here tonight to give it a horsey smell instead of ours. Then let's get to bed."

Blythe's head had hardly fallen back on her pillow when she was roused by a vigorous shake and her father's excited whisper.

"Blythe! Dan! The mare's in the corral with Dick. Come on and let's pen her in quick!"

To the girl's surprise it was dark no longer and the Pocket had a lid of silver blue over it. The sun was not yet in sight although it glowed on the highest peaks. She scrambled into her clothes and started toward the gate, afraid to move too fast lest her uneven gait frighten the buckskin out of her trap. Blythe circled around in order to come in from the angle of the gate, while Dan and Mr. Hyland were making a bigger circle, but Dark Sunshine was already aware of their presence and moved around nervously inside the corral. Blythe took as big a breath as her efforts permitted and launched into "When I'm calling you" which briefly deflected the mare's interest from the men.

The girl babbled a breathless combination of words and songs, not daring to spare a hand from her crutch to whistle, but her delaying action had been successful. She reached the gap in the fence before Dark Sunshine made a break for it. Blythe stood there, panting from her exertions, but getting into position lulled her into a false security.

Dark Sunshine was not so alarmed by Blythe's presence, but the instant the men came into view the mare knew she must make a dash for her freedom and she charged for the gateway which was barred only by the girl's slight figure. Blythe yelled and waved her hat at the plunging horse that by now was insensible with fright.

Dan saw his sister's danger and knew in a flash she'd never give ground. Scooping up a handful of pebbles he shot forward as if from a starting line, yelling like a madman, and when even this failed to halt the charging mare, he let fly with a handful of stones. A few hit Blythe who never felt them but most of them went over her head, struck Dark Sunshine full in the face and made her wheel and rush back into the corral where she crowded behind Dick.

"Whew! I feel kind of weak in my crutches," Blythe laughed shakily. "She sure wanted out!"

"Well, goon, why didn't you get out of the way?" Dan exploded angrily. "Keep on fussing around like that and you'll have a one-way trip to the morgue."

"Good heavens, Blythe, what were you planning to do? Wrestle her even Stephen and no holds barred?" her father snorted. "I don't know whether you're to be trusted with a horse after all."

"It just happened so suddenly I couldn't believe she'd really run me down. Hers was a case of temporary insanity from fright. Once we're acquainted I'm sure she'd never do it."

Mr. Hyland and Dan slapped a gate together in record time and stoutly fastened it in place. At first Dark Sunshine was beside herself when she found there was no escape from the men and she plunged back and forth in the far end of the corral until even old Dick was aroused and but for his hobbles would have raced around like a yearling.

Finding that no harm had come to her, the mare finally quieted down and was content to watch the activity from a safe position behind Dick, her head over his back. Blythe went around to a spot on the far side only a few feet from the buckskin, and talked and whistled to calm her, but other than an occasional backward flip of an ear the mare ignored her.

Breakfast that morning should have been a triumphant feast. The trail was more than half repaired. The mare was penned though still a long way from gentled, but a nagging unhappiness rode in Blythe's stomach like an uneasy meal.

"Da-a-ad," she said tentatively.

"Oh, oh! What now? That tone of yours means bad news," he replied in high spirits.

"No, not necessarily, but I would like to do a little dickering with you—though I'm hardly in a strong enough position to drive much of a bargain. But, Dad, Sunny's never been roughed up and never had any cause to mistrust us two-legged animals. You and Dan will be busy on the trail all day so just give me today to work with her and if I don't make any progress, then you can rope her. Please?"

"That'll keep us here longer, sugar."

"It might not. There are hours and hours yet today, and if I don't win, roping and haltering her won't take very long. Please, please, Dad. I know she'll be sensible about it!"

"Even if it did take us an extra day, Dad, we'd be pretty well paid for our time," Dan, the peacemaker, interposed. "Dark Sunshine must be worth several hundred dollars and that'd be pretty good pay for amateurs," he grinned.

"That's so. I hadn't thought of that," Blythe was dumfounded at his calculations. "I've been thinking of her just as a horse I wanted so much I could hardly stand it, but she does have a value, doesn't she?"

"She certainly does," her father nodded, "and it was pretty nice of 'Also' to sign off like he did. Well, ten years from now I suppose it won't matter if we do take an extra day. Go ahead, Blythe. Have your fun, but don't get yourself hurt!"

"I won't, Dad. I promise. I'll be extra careful. Think I'll wait until you two are out of sight before trying to make up to her. Then she won't have anything else on her mind."

Blythe rubbed pieces of chestnut over her hands with such passionate thoroughness she smelled more like a horse than a horse would and her pockets bulged with delicacies designed to tempt the equine appetite. She wore a short length of rope around her shoulders like a scarf and in her free hand she carried a halter and a longer rope.

Thus armed, she headed for the corral the minute the men turned toward the trail. Dark Sunshine watched Blythe's approach with more interest than alarm and when she slid into the corral the buckskin snuffed mightily at the good smells that wafted toward her.

The girl leaned comfortably in a corner and softly crooned song after song to her alert audience. At last the mare stepped from behind buffer Dick and faced her. Blythe reverted to low-voiced conversation and even resorted to a little hypnotism, trying to hold the mare's eyes with her own, while her hand displayed a lump of sugar.

A black hoof moved forward, then another, and another, until Dark Sunshine had passed the center of the corral. There she halted and neither words nor promised rewards budged her. Blythe shot a calculating glance at the sun and was relieved to see that it was only midmorning.

"Lucky thing you did get us up so early, girl. It gives me a lot more time for this, but, oh, please do come closer!"

Blythe's determination increased, but her words were as soft, as gentle as ever. Her hand rocked the white cube invitingly, but it might have been a white pebble for all the attention the mare paid it.

Blythe grew more and more desperate as the minutes passed and Dark Sunshine made no further move. The strain of absolute immobility except for an outstretched arm began to tell and the girl slowly dropped her arm to her side. Still motionless she considered what should be her next move, but it was the buckskin that made it.

When Blythe's voice and wooing ceased, it was as though the mare grew worried that the offer might be withdrawn. Ears pricked straight front, she minced forward cautiously. Farther and farther she came and instead of growing more nervous, Dark Sunshine seemed to take confidence from the girl's nearness. The last few feet were covered slowly—to the taut girl they seemed to take hours—but at last the buckskin was no farther than an arm's length away.

The delicate nostrils ruffled soundlessly as the inquisitive mare investigated the delightful aromas from her new friend. Slowly, slowly, an arm stretched out to offer the lump of sugar. The buckskin nearly whuffed it off the cupped palm, but once identified as the delicacy of the day before her lips picked it up daintily. A moment later, Blythe offered her a handful of grain. That, she decided at once, was worth closer acquaintance and she took the final step forward to be rewarded by another handful.

After that the storehouse door was closed and the eager mare grew bolder and bolder in her search for more. With a steadiness that belied her inner turmoil, Blythe offered a handful of grain with the arm that leaned on her crutch while she laid her other hand with gentle firmness on the golden neck.

Blythe could feel the tremor in the mare at this first alien touch but she whistled softly between her teeth to soothe her. Then she slid her hand under the flared Arabian jawbones and scratched with a light pressure. This made Dark Sunshine stretch her neck and twitch her upper lip in sheer delight.

Afterward Blythe could never tell just how long she stood by the greedy buckskin, doling out stingy dabs of grain, her hands roving lightly over the neck and head, before she slipped the short rope from her own shoulders and eased one end softly around the golden neck. It seemed to feel much the same to the mare as Blythe's touch and the girl was soon able to move the rope about. Then, holding the two loose ends in her hand, she pulled gently. The dainty head gave slightly in answer and emboldened by her success Blythe increased her pressure. Her exultation was hard to repress when the mare's head and neck moved in either direction at the rope's behest.

Dark Sunshine was rewarded with a generous portion of grain and as she munched it, Blythe replaced the rope with the rope halter. When the mare turned toward her for more, the girl complied, holding her hand so that the mare's nose went into the halter. It was nosed aside impatiently and before long

the mare considered it only an impediment that came between
her and her tidbits.

For the final stroke Blythe planted herself firmly so that
she was in no danger of losing her balance and frightening
the mare. While the mare munched two lumps of sugar,
Blythe eased the nose band into place, and fastened the throat
latch. Her dream horse was haltered. The girl's brown hands
caressed and scratched as a counterirritant until the buckskin
became aware of her changed condition but except for a few
nervous tosses of her head there were no hard feelings.

Scraping the bottom of her pockets Blythe fed the mare
the last of her supplies as a distraction while she snapped the
longer drag rope in the halter ring. This long, snakey-looking
thing was not to Dark Sunshine's liking and she danced backward several steps, snorting and spooking as the rope trailed
her.

"You've got to be pretty well rope-broken before we dare
try to take you out of here, Sunny, and dragging one's the
best and fastest way. Please don't take it too hard. Now all of
a sudden I'm hungry but you oughtn't to be, you've been eating since sun-up."

Blythe left the corral and headed for camp and lunch, to be
greeted by a joyous hail.

"You win, skeeter. If I hadn't seen it, I'd never have believed it," Mr. Hyland exclaimed and his daughter suddenly
wondered how long they had been watching from the trail.
"That's your grandfather all over again. He could go into a
corral with the wildest broomtail you ever saw and subdue
him by just looking him in the eye, it seemed. Always wished

I could too but it never worked for me. To think that it skipped me and now crops up in you!"

"You sure put the hex on her, Butch. Wow! What a Houdini you'd make."

"Ah-h, you're both being silly. Besides I haven't told you about my secret trick. This." She showed them her pieces of magic. "I remembered from someplace that rubbing hunks of a horse's chestnut on your hands was a trick Indians used —so I tried it."

"Missing no bets, eh?" her father said with a laugh. "I've heard of old-timers using asafetida."

"Is that so! I'll remember that for my next wild horse!"

"Yes, you will—*not!*" Mr. Hyland countered. "Come on, we'd better get Dick out of there to make sure he isn't tangled up in that rope."

When her father and Dan returned to their work, Blythe happily went back to the corral. She was alarmed to find that the halter and rope had apparently disturbed the mare, for she paced the corral, looking longingly over the top at the open spaces she had lost. Blythe fought a hard battle with herself, thinking that her prize was already yearning for her liberty, until the brook and a sunbeam tipped her the wink.

"You're thirsty! That's your trouble. It's *Water, Cool Water* you're singing instead of *Don't Fence Me In*. Well, I know just the stuff for that but you'll have to be patient while I get it."

The girl managed to get back to the buckskin with the pail more than half full of water but then its strangeness repelled Dark Sunshine. Blythe cupped her hands in the water and let it trickle through her fingers enticingly, at which the mare pawed her aggravation. Thirst won out, however, and Blythe triumphantly held the pail while her dream horse drank.

Their afternoon together passed happily for both horse and girl as they came to know each other better and better. Dick too joined them as soon as his hunger was satisfied and, slouched off on one hip, he drowsed in the shade just outside the fence.

When friendly relations seemed firmly established Blythe took the trailing end of the rope, gently moved it around, and found that it bothered the mare very little. The girl walked up it halfway and then stood still, a lump of sugar in one hand, the other giving little jerks to the rope as she said a peremptory "Come!" Dark Sunshine understood one signal if not the other, soon associating it with a forward movement, and she followed her limping friend through several varied patterns.

Mr. Hyland and Dan were later than usual that evening and Blythe had supper ready before they returned to the Pocket. She had been thrilled to have Dark Sunshine put her head over the bars and look after her when she finally pulled herself away from the corral, so the minute supper preparations were complete Blythe took a seat facing the corral and treated the mare to another concert.

"Haven't heard you do so much singing in years as you've done in the past couple of days, hon. Why save that nice voice of yours for horses?" Her father tousled her hair affectionately before dropping beside their campfire.

"You see it's kind of a letter of introduction and I think I know you two pretty well already. Tell you what though. After supper, as soon as I can cut some grass for Sunny, I'll favor you with a request program—but we'll have it at the corral. OK?"

"The very thing. We've finished the trail and now all we need is a certain amount of co-operation from your new friend. The sooner she gets to know Dan and me better, the sooner we can go home."

"Oh, that won't take long. We've made wonderful progress. She'll already let me lead her around!"

Blythe spared scant attention for their report that the trail was complete, and supper conversation revolved around the wonder horse. Dan and his father had to admit their astonishment when they saw what good terms Blythe and Sunny were on, but that it did not extend to the two men was evident. At the girl's insistence, however, they entered the corral and made themselves comfortable for her request concert.

Dark Sunshine skittered off to the farthest corner of the enclosure and watched them fearfully, but as one song led into the next she relaxed her vigilance slightly. She snapped alert whenever either of them moved, but she was losing the sharp edge to her fear by the time Blythe sang *Home on the Range* for her closing number.

"Tomorrow will be a 'Sunny day' for sure. We'll spend it working with the mare, getting her used to us, and early the next morning we'll plan to start for home." Her father's declaration startled some of Blythe's fears into the open.

"How are we going to do it? Suppose she won't make up that soon. What if she puts up a fight?"

"She'll be ready," Mr. Hyland said flatly. "We can't take any longer and if she won't come peacefully, we'll have to persuade her to our way of doing things. I think she'll be pretty sensible about it though, so don't worry."

XI: Empty Pocket

AFTER HOURS of working and wooing Dark Sunshine Mr. Hyland and Dan were not such fearsome objects to her but she made it plain that if she had a choice it was Blythe she preferred. Dick proved well worth any extra trouble he might have caused, for his was a steadying presence that the mare often used as a buffer.

Blythe's father looked more and more concerned as the day wore along and it became clearer and clearer that the buckskin would make plenty of trouble for him and Dan. One thing their attentions had done was to make the bond between horse and girl even closer but that was scant comfort with a long, steep trail ahead.

"Well, if she wants to be so chummy with you and Dick,
let's see how you'd make out. We'll saddle Dick and let him
stand in there a bit while she gets used to the leather smells
and then you three can take a trial spin."

"Outside the corral, Dad? Suppose she should get away?"

"If she's going to, now's the time to find out and not when
we're all crowded onto a narrow trail. I think she'll be all
right with you two though, and now that we have a halter
on her, you'll have better control."

Once the preliminaries had been completed and Blythe
was mounted on Dick she felt more confident. Reining him
over toward Dark Sunshine, she was content to sit and talk
for a few minutes while she doled out a continuing stream of
small tidbits until the mare accepted the elevated position.
Then Blythe quietly took up the trailing rope which she dallied around the saddle horn and set Dick into a walk.

Several sharp commands of "Come" and a slight vibration
of the rope reminded Dark Sunshine of her previous day's
lesson and except for one jerk when she pulled back, confused by the faster pace, she readily fell in with the plan.
Blythe guided Dick back and forth and around the corral
until she felt certain that the mare knew what was expected
of her, then nodded to her helpers that she was ready to try
it on a larger scale.

The gate was swung open and Blythe and Dick, with Sunny
alongside, stepped out into the Pocket proper. One look at
the open spaces before her and the mare lunged forward but

Blythe had expected some such shenanigan and kept a tight dally around the horn that foiled the would-be escape.

"Easy, Sunny, easy. There's no use getting yourself all excited. I've got you right by that little head of yours, by the nose in fact, and it gives me quite an advantage."

To reassure the fretting horse that jigged nervously beside her Blythe whistled softly through her teeth. Staid Dick's example and many minutes of quiet walking had a good effect on Dark Sunshine and before returning to the corral, Blythe had the satisfaction of seeing the mare steady down and follow docilely.

"That's my girl. Slow and easy does it and we'll get along fine."

Blythe punctuated her approval with another lump of sugar and as an additional guarantee of good conduct, the girl guided her mount back into the corral, around a few times and out again. This exit was more mannerly and the girl was satisfied with a short circle that led back to the gate.

"Good girls, both of you," her father greeted them. "Looks like the best way is for you and Dick to play bellwether tomorrow when we leave. With Dan ahead of you and me behind, I think the mare'll be content to just tag along with you —and it'll save Dan a trip up for the other horses."

"But the pack, Dad. What about that?"

"We'll just have to be pack horses ourselves. Not much left but our bedrolls and tools and that's no more than many a mountain climber has to tote."

The next morning Dick was saddled and Blythe repeated the preceding day's routine, even to a short trip out into the

Pocket to make sure that Dark Sunshine remembered her lessons. She proved to be letter perfect.

"Better hold the rope with your left hand, hon, so you can keep your back to the wall if you have to turn in your saddle," her father advised casually on reaching the foot of the trail. "Looks like there'll soon be another empty Pocket on the Lazy SL."

The girl half expected Dark Sunshine to put up some argument at the beginning of the climb but she followed willingly. Not until they reached the point where the slide had been did she try to hang back.

"I'll bet she's tried the trail up this far many a time when her loneliness got too much to bear," Blythe exclaimed in sudden understanding. "Well, come along, girlie, it's just more of the same—a lot more!"

Their ascent was slow and apparently endless. The foot company with packs found it necessary to rest frequently and as the sun and the temperature rose, the rest stops increased. Patient, plodding Dick was not having an easy time either with a heavy saddle and rider on top and a roped convoy behind that halted suddenly at the most awkward moments. The cavalcade's line-up had been based on the fact that the mare was warier of Mr. Hyland than of Dan, and whenever she showed signs of hanging back Blythe's father had only to speak to remind her of his presence and she stepped out smartly.

"Glory be! Aren't we nearly there yet, Dan?" Blythe asked during a breather.

"Yes—we're about half way. What are you worrying about? You've got a cinch."

"That's what you think. This is really harder on me because of the mental anguish I'm suffering for the rest of you. I've been thinking though that I'm going to do something nice for all of you—you too, Dickie old boy." She tapped the sweaty shoulder. "Oh, I can't tell you what," she hastily added, "in fact, I don't know just what myself yet. But it'll be extra nice, so you can be thinking about it as you climb."

Blythe's smile was half promise and half tease. In the meantime there was still a long climb ahead and when Dan rose to his feet she brought her mind back to the present.

They climbed and stopped and climbed and stopped until Blythe lost all track of time. She was, therefore, genuinely surprised when the trail leveled off and she found herself in the scrub growth at the top of the draw.

Blythe dismounted briefly to rest herself as well as her horse, and her father snubbed Dark Sunshine around a tree. Meanwhile Dan had saddled their horses and laid out their unpretentious lunch so all three were soon in the saddle again on the home stretch. Mounted, they retained the same order of march, Dan ahead, Blythe and Dick with Sunny in the middle and Mr. Hyland with the pack horse bringing up the rear.

Dark Sunshine was not so shy of the men once they were a-horseback. Her instincts had told her that there were horses like herself in the world and she was in an excited lather at meeting the others. They too were on tiptoe at seeing a pretty young mare and there was much nickering and neck-stretching at first.

Mrs. Hyland had no way of knowing what day the horse-hunting trio would be coming home and was, therefore, unable to meet Blythe with the truck, but the past few days had accomplished miracles in hardening and conditioning her. Even if she had been physically exhausted the anticipated thrill of leading her new horse into the home yard would have buoyed her up.

"This has been the most wonderful experience in my whole life, but it's going to be nice to sleep in a bed for a change, isn't it?" she said in totaling up the debits and credits.

"Yes, and for once I've had my fill of pancakes and bacon— not that I mean to criticize your cooking, Blythe. You did fine with what we had."

"Wouldn't it be a joke on us if Mom planned to have pancakes and bacon for a quick supper?" Dan chuckled, borrowing trouble.

"She'd never—of course, she wouldn't! She knows what we took with us."

Blythe sat very straight in the saddle when the little pack train turned into the driveway. The mare had been nervously snapping her ears back and forth as she saw one strange sight after another, and the girl made a quick mental note to give her mother a big hug for keeping herself and the children indoors. Blythe could see them with their noses pressed against the window.

The yard was still and silent except for the sound of their horses' hoofs and Blythe's low-voiced reassurances. Dan had increased his lead in order to open the gates and, hoping that the lead rope did not betray her shaking hands, Blythe guided Dick and Sunny through the wide gate into the large corral.

"Gotcha this far anyway," she crowed. "Now one more

gate and you'll be in your own little place. Come along, girlie."

Blythe's words or Dark Sunshine's instincts warned her that gates and fences meant bondage. She held back on the rope and Blythe obligingly eased up to give her time to think it over, but a second firm pressure was futile. The girl searched her pockets hopefully but not a single tidbit could she find for bribery so she again tried to coax the buckskin through.

The mare's ears slanted outward from her head in a stubborn expression accented by her firmly placed forefeet. She did not choose to enter, and Blythe knew the longer they tried the more determined would be Dark Sunshine's opposition, but in facing the gate so stubbornly the mare had completely forgotten Mr. Hyland. He sneaked up dead behind her on her blind spot.

"Hi-yahhh!" he yelled suddenly, slapping his thigh with his hat.

Through the round corral gate in one bound went the mare, Dick and Blythe following like the tail of a comet. The gate was clapped shut behind them and at last Dark Sunshine was safely penned at the Lazy SL. She raced around the corral, head up and tail so high the black hairs fell forward across her golden quarters.

Blythe and Dick held to the center, a safe enough position since the mare was circling the fence. The kitchen door banged and Chris and Amy came dashing toward the barn pell-mell, followed by Mrs. Hyland at a more respectable pace.

"Slow down, kids! Come quietly or she might go over the fence," Blythe yelled frantically.

"Go on back to the house if you haven't any more sense than that," her father roared in support.

One command or the other restored their senses and like two little lambs they walked up beside their mother to look round-eyed at the new horse. Dark Sunshine looked every bit as beautiful as advance reports had made them expect. Chris, of course, had seen her from a distance but even he was dazzled by her perfection.

She slowed down gradually a notch at a time and, when Dan brought her an armful of cured hay, the first she had ever had, hunger overcame fear and she ate greedily. Blythe rode Dick over to the gate where she dismounted. Dan unsaddled for her and the old horse was left with the mare for company.

The six Hylands stared through the fence at Blythe's new horse and each admired or envied as nature determined. Though Dark Sunshine was eating, every nerve was alert, and, seizing a mouthful of hay, she chewed it nervously with her head high, watching for danger.

"Morgan and Arabian makes a nice breeding blend," Mrs. Hyland said judiciously. "You couldn't fault her any place at all."

"She'll make a perfect stock horse with Arabian quickness and Morgan stamina," Mr. Hyland agreed. "Take a lot of training though."

"How soon're you going to ride her, Blythe?" Amy asked, wide-eyed.

"That you'll have to ask her, sugar. She knows the answer better than I do."

"One thing leads to another," Chris jibed. "Now you have

a horse of your own but no saddle. What'll you do about that?"

"I'll use yours!" Blythe knew that would silence her young brother, at least for the moment.

"You won't have to, Butch," Dan added quickly before Chris's gathering storm broke. "I found an old Mexican saddletree in the barn junk and I've fixed it up so I think it'll be easier for you to ride than one of those stiff, heavy stock saddles."

"Dan, you angel! I'll have to think of something extra, extra nice to do for you." Blythe squeezed his arm warmly.

"That was sure thoughtful of you, son." Mrs. Hyland added her approval. "Bring it out and let's have a look at it."

Dan disappeared into the barn and came out with a burlap sack from which he drew a dilapidated old saddle. The rawhide-covered tree gave mute evidence of years of use and the stirrup leathers and patched rigging were of varying shades of color. Only the girth was new and its brightness made the other parts shabbier by contrast.

Blythe looked it over happily, glad to have a saddle all her own, yet somehow disappointed in its looks. It certainly wouldn't add to Sunny's beauty. To cover her feelings she leaned over to pick it up, bracing herself for the weight, but she could lift it with one hand.

"Why, it hardly weighs anything. I can saddle my own horse," she cried in genuine delight. "Now I can do everything for myself!"

XII: Burlap Jockey

N O LONGER did Blythe's parents have any trouble getting her out-of-doors. Their difficulties, if any, were encountered in getting her back indoors and away from Dark Sunshine's corral where the girl was content to just stand and stare when there was nothing more to do for the mare.

For the first day or two Dan or his father always happened to be nearby until Sunny's disposition proved to be as good as her name and her sweet temper and gentleness became more and more evident. Blythe's interest was Dan's interest at any time, however, and he spent as much time with her and her horse as he could spare from his ranch work, for he realized that there would be many times his help would be needed and the better the mare knew him the easier it would be.

Dark Sunshine slowly came to accept the other Hylands, but because Blythe was the first human being who had paid her attention she had an advantage that could never be surpassed. Even her handicap was helpful in a way as it enforced a slowness and deliberation in their relationship that a more active person might have forgotten at times, and the buckskin seemed to know that her friend was not as spry as herself. She stepped carefully when she moved and the curious nosing that was such a part of their growing friendship was softly and gently done.

If the mare resisted any new move, whether from fright or incomplete understanding, Blythe was patience plus. Sunny's first lesson had taught her that their whistle meant her friend was coming and in a short time the alert horse could pick Blythe's voice out of a six-Hyland conversation and prove it with a welcoming whinny.

Dark Sunshine's first week at the Lazy SL was devoted entirely to gentling and getting better acquainted, but then Blythe began to fret that the mare wasn't getting enough exercise in the small corral. Dick was still her only close four-footed friend and it was considered too risky to turn her into the horse pasture yet.

"We could teach her to go on a longe line," the girl tentatively suggested. "It oughtn't to be hard. The corral's round to start with and it's time to start her training anyway."

"What about the snubbing post in the center, hon? Mightn't that get in your way?"

"I wouldn't think so, Dad. There's a certain amount of

milling around at first and I can just inch around the post while I'm at it."

"It certainly won't hurt to try. You and Dan might have a go at it after supper and if it doesn't work out, I'll come and give you a hand."

By now the rope held no threat for the buckskin and she watched their preparations with great interest. Her calm was unruffled until Dan haltered Dick and led him through the gate. Then Dark Sunshine would have rushed after him. Finding her exit barred she raced up and down the fence in great excitement, and only by tying the old horse just outside were they able to quiet the bereaved mare.

"Wish I could be the one to lead her along at first, Dan, but I'm afraid I'd be more of a drag," Blythe said matter-of-factly. "I'll just have to be anchor man on this team."

She planted herself by the snubbing post, a long switch in her right hand, her left holding the rope paid out enough for Dark Sunshine to stand by the fence with one ear cocked at Dan who stood beside her.

"Walk!" Dan and Blythe cracked simultaneously with their characteristic one-ness.

Dan suited action to word and his right hand on the halter pressed forward. Sunny obeyed, but half a circuit was the most she could manage at a walk and her tickling heels picked up a trot. Blythe was so enthralled by the beautiful action she almost forgot her duties. One breathless circle was all Dan could keep up so he retreated along the line to the center.

As the mare wore off her first burst of energy she would have lagged but Dan slipped outward again to spur her on. Once she had been taught the feeling that she was doing it because they wanted it and not just because it pleased her, she was stopped, praised and reversed. Some of the bounce had gone out of her legs by then and Dan was able to regulate her pace more easily.

Her wild life had kept her in good condition and the light work-out in the corral hardly made her turn a hair but Blythe insisted on a slower pace to cool her out. Dan no longer needed to hold the rope and just strolling along midway between horse and girl and a little to the rear maintained the desired gait.

"I think she's catching on wonderfully well. Don't you, Dan?"

"Yep, I sure do. She's smart all right, and if you can keep her trusting you, she'll make a winner."

To relieve the monotony of many circuits of the corral, all at a walk with occasional direction changes, they talked in snatches but the subject was always Dark Sunshine. Indoors there was little change in their topic.

"She's coming along so well, Dad, she'll be ready for saddling before we know it."

"It hadn't better be before *I* know it. I'm not going to have you kids try to ride her the first time. It's too risky."

"Dad! *You're* not! I want to be the only one to ever ride Sunny."

There was anguish in Blythe's voice and heart to think that someone else, even her father, might be the first to ride her dream horse.

"But, Blythe honey, you don't think that you could top her off first time, do you? You're a good little horseman but you aren't a bronc rider. It's a different style altogether." Her father felt his way carefully, fearful lest he blast this first all-absorbing interest of hers, yet more fearful of what too great ambition might get her into.

"Sunny isn't a bronc. She's sweet and gentle and has never known anything but kindness and I'm sure she wouldn't hurt me once she's progressed to where she's ready for riding. But she's got spirit and fire, and treating her like a bronc might make her one."

Mr. Hyland's brain was in a whirl. What to say? What to do? For once he welcomed Chris's sally.

"Blythe Hyland, aren't you even going to let me ride your old horse?"

"Not even you, sonny boy. Fate has sent me a fresh, unspoiled horse and I intend to keep her all mine. My toothbrush you can use any time you want to, but my horse, no!"

That silenced them temporarily when they saw how much it meant to the girl, and her father decided for the moment to retreat in good order.

"No use getting all worked up about it now anyway. There's still a lot of work to be done on her before she'll be anywhere near ready to ride."

After that family crisis Blythe redoubled her attentions to the mare and many strange and unusual objects were carried along for Sunny's appraisal. First the girl began carrying a folded feed sack across her shoulders and the lingering aroma of grain was its passport to acceptance. That hazard passed, Blythe unfolded the sack and waved it around more freely. The mare snorted and dodged at first but, finding no harm resulted, she soon ignored it. Early in their relationship Blythe's caresses had been emphasized by brush strokes and as soon as possible the sack was utilized as another grooming tool and rubbed back and forth on the mare's glossy coat. Eventually, of course, it rested lightly across her back.

With that step accepted, one day Blythe passed the rope shank over the sack and caught it under the mare's belly. Slowly, softly it was drawn up so that she felt its pressure around her body. Her ears pointed backward and the white of one eye showed as she turned to see what was going on.

"Something on your mind, Sunny?" Blythe asked with a caress in her voice. "Or is it what's on your back that's bothering you?"

The pressure was released for that lesson, only to be repeated the next day and the next. From time to time, Blythe would put an arm across the mare's golden back, patting her and resting what weight she could there.

One evening when Dan was through helping his father, he and Blythe fitted Dark Sunshine to the hackamore. It was little different from the halter to which she was accustomed, with one strand of rawhide over the ears as a headstall and another large loop of braided rawhide slipped over the nose something like a cavesson. The horsehair reins were attached by a large knot under the chin, and the throatlatch, or fiador, secured it all in place.

"Can't do much with that until she's wearing a saddle to loop the rein over," Blythe muttered, "but it won't be long. I'm certainly glad that saddle you made for me is so light. I don't think she'll mind it half as much as a regular stock saddle."

"Dad's weighs a ton. What if she has to get used to that one?"

"She won't. Mine'll be all she'll need to worry about."

"Or shall we say, all *you* need to worry about?" Dan countered, content to be only a spectator of the impending battle of wills.

Sunny's acceptance of the feed sack meant the last of it and a folded blanket replaced it. This was held on by a broad strip of webbing which the girl carefully tightened a little more each day and as soon as it was snug enough to stay in place the buckskin wore it during her longeing.

These lessons went along rapidly and proved that she was ready and willing to learn. The walk and trot on command were easily mastered and with Dan an extra anchor Dark Sunshine was sent into a canter. At first it was a snappy affair and she whizzed around the corral like a rock in a sling, but control won out and she settled down to a gentle lope.

Watching the horse cantering around, the blanket strapped in place, a terrible longing to be able to vault onto her back as a bareback rider would or to make a cowboy's flying mount swept Blythe. She was so mesmerized by the dizzying circles that for one wild moment she felt she could, until the jab of her crutch wakened her to reality.

The next day when Sunny was to be longed, Dan brought the new-old saddle down to the corral. Taking off the flapping stirrups, the mare was invited to sniff it thoroughly and this was followed by a series of gentle movements. In a short time Dark Sunshine gave it scant attention and at a nod from Blythe, Dan set the saddle on the blanketed back.

Sunny knew she was carrying something heavier than her former load though it was not especially irksome. She fidgeted a little but Dan slapped her shoulder to distract her thoughts from her back and Blythe gave her a lump of sugar which completely eclipsed other considerations. Without giving her a chance to worry about the new development, the buckskin was put into her longeing routine.

"Goes just like a lamb, doesn't she, Dan?"

"That she does. 'Twon't be any time before she'll be ready to ride. That canter of hers looks better'n a rocking chair."

"I can hardly wait to ride her, but I'll have to hurry or Dad'll beat me to it."

That thought was always in the back of Blythe's mind to spur her on. Neither weariness nor her other chores kept her from seeing that Sunny had her training each day, and in reward the mare shaped up faster than Blythe had dared to hope. Not so many lessons after her first under the stripped-down saddle the stirrups were attached and tied down to keep their flapping from frightening the mare.

Anything that Blythe could devise that might further the horse's education was tried, generally successfully, for the girl's instincts about her horse seemed infallible, but after a while even she ran out of things to do except more of the same. Dark Sunshine longed perfectly under hackamore and full saddle with loose stirrups. She stopped on command and picked up any of her three gaits at a word and backed true as a rule.

"All she needs is a rider, Sis."

Blythe thrilled to Dan's words which expressed her own feelings. She nibbled thoughtfully on a mesquite bean.

"Well, I guess we could manage that too, if we tried."

"Butch, don't you dare or Dad'll be mighty mad. He might

even say you couldn't keep the mare for disobeying him like that!"

"Oh, I didn't mean me. Why couldn't we put some sand in a grain sack and set it on her back. Every day or two we could put a little more sand in it to build up the weight gradually and presto! after a bit it'd be just like me there. Sometimes I think I ride like a sack of sand anyway." Blythe giggled.

"How'll we keep it in place? A sack of sand hasn't much horsemanship in it."

"You walk beside her and hold it on! That'll get her used to your being there for when I get on—and you'll be ready to catch me in case she goes to pieces at the feeling of live weight."

On matters that concerned Sunny there was little lag between Blythe's thinking and acting. The same old sack Sunny knew was scooped about a quarter full of sand and eased into the saddle. With so much slack Dan was able to fasten it by the corners and the mare was put through a modified longeing lesson with little to mar its smoothness.

"She's used to my legs already. Here go my hips and waist," Blythe said the following day as Dan prepared to lift the half-full sack onto the horse.

Dark Sunshine noticed the added weight and tossed her head fretfully though there was no suggestion of a hump in her back. Again Dan could secure the sack tight enough for a few circuits at a walk. Once the buckskin jigged a step or two and her ears flattened tight at the unaccustomed thuds when the bag jogged up and down.

In view of her reactions to the half-full bag, the same routine was repeated several days and she had accepted the strange burden completely before more sand was added. Dan gave an extra grunt when he heaved the three-quarters-full sack of sand into the saddle which he followed with several sighs as he strode beside the fast-walking mare to hold the burlap jockey in place.

"Well, there're my legs and hips and waist and chest now," Blythe commented with satisfaction. "My, what a big girl I'm getting to be, eh, Sunny?"

More days elapsed to give the mare a chance to become accustomed to her growing jockey, but then she was ready for the complete load.

"We'll have to make your head and shoulders a little smaller than life-size to be sure there's enough slack in the bag. If it's too full it'd be pretty hard to hold on—it'll be hard enough to set it on. But here goes!"

Dan hoisted the sack to his shoulders and thence across the saddle. So used was Dark Sunshine to the strange weight on her back she paid little attention to the increase and walked around the corral docilely. Several lessons more and her training was as complete as possible without a real rider, and Blythe looked longingly at the empty saddle.

XIII: The Will to Do

BEFORE BLYTHE could tell her father at suppertime of Dark Sunshine's readiness, he announced that he would need all his riders for two or three days on ranch work. Blythe had not been away from the ranch house since their return from the Pocket and the prospect of a long ride made her forget her intentions.

"Better get to bed in good season, kids. I want to get started early before the cattle have a chance to bush up."

"Bush up, Daddy? Don't you mean 'brush up'?" Amy queried.

"No, sweetheart, I don't. Just offhand I don't see how a cow could brush up, but they bush up as soon as it begins to get hot—they find a likely clump of bushes and lie down in the shade. That makes it twice as hard to find them as when they're on their feet grazing."

Blythe felt like a traitor the next morning when Sunny nickered at her approach, only to see Dick saddled and led out of their joint quarters. The girl took time for a soft pat and a few love words, made sweeter with some sugar, but nothing altered the fact that she rode away on another horse and left Dark Sunshine all alone for hours.

The next day was little different although Blythe managed to give Sunny her longeing after supper. That completed, the girl sat on the top rail awhile and talked to the buckskin. To Dick too, for he had joined the select group, but for once Sunny made it plain he was not welcome and whenever he stopped beneath Blythe's feet he was soon jostled out of the way.

"I do believe you're getting jealous of your old friend, Sunny. That's not very nice of you."

Blythe leaned over and stroked the golden arch of neck and, content to have won the favored position, the mare basked in the warmth of the girl's affection. A third day of loneliness and neglect while her boss was away on upstart Dick was more than Dark Sunshine proposed to tolerate, however. When she saw him saddled and Blythe prepared to mount, with ears back and teeth bared, she flew at him in a rage.

"Dad! Dad, look here a minute if you think Sunny wouldn't let me ride her. She's jealous as anything of Dick and doesn't want me to even get on him. Now watch this. Hold him a sec, Dan."

Blythe walked up to the wild-eyed Dick, the innocent decoy. She picked up the reins and went through several false mounting motions which brought Dark Sunshine down on them again like a wolf on a tethered lamb. So furious were the mare's tactics, Dick was finally led through the gate and Blythe mounted on the other side.

"Now do you understand when I say she wants to carry me? Last night when I was perched on the fence, she kept driving Dick away from in front of me so she'd be in position for me to get on. A plainer invitation I never saw. Can't I try it just once, Dad? Please."

Her father was out of his depth and knew it, so he stalled for time and reinforcements.

"How can you be sure that's what she means? Maybe it's saddles she hates."

"Oh, no, that isn't it, Dad!" Blythe recounted the mare's progress and how tractable she had been at every step and Dan nodded confirmation. Their father then took refuge in a delaying action.

"We'll see what your mother says. And anyway we have to go to town tomorrow."

Once again Blythe would have begged off going to town with the others but this time her presence was required.

"It's for your six-month check-up, dear," her mother explained. "Your other doctor gave us Dr. Harrison's name and last week we made an appointment for you. Don't worry, Sunny will be all right."

Both her father and mother accompanied her for this first visit to a new doctor. He was tall and graying and genial, Blythe discovered, and somehow managed to seem both professionally competent and sympathetic as a friend. The three

Hylands were ushered into his office where they sat and talked with him awhile as he occasionally referred to a folder which Blythe recognized as the same one her other doctor had had.

The examination took but a short time and, closing the connecting door, the doctor returned to his office where Mr. and Mrs. Hyland waited. Blythe continued dressing, turning as she heard the latch click. No one entered but a breeze which brought with it the three-way conversation.

". . . and I find it hard to believe it's the same girl these records pertain to," she heard Dr. Harrison saying. "What exercises has she been taking to effect such a marked improvement?"

Blythe heard her mother and father collaborating on her story and she wondered uneasily whether she should cough or tell them the door was unlatched.

"They ought to know it as well as I do," she reasoned, "and besides, I'm the party of the first part!"

"Splendid! I prescribe more of the same," the doctor was saying. "Her crutches look as though one hadn't been used as much as the other. Does she sometimes use just one?"

Blythe heard the murmur of her parents' affirmatives.

"Good. She ought to discard the other one then. There's nothing worse than using an artificial support when it's no longer needed. Do you have any questions you would like to ask?"

There was a short silence, broken by Mr. Hyland's deep tones. Blythe involuntarily stopped lacing her shoe as her father recounted her absorption with Dark Sunshine and she froze motionless when he came to the conclusion.

"Now the mare's ready to ride, yet she doesn't want anyone else to ride her. We're afraid to have her try it, though I must admit the buckskin is as gentle as a kitten with her and those two kids have done everything possible to have her ready for it. I don't know what to say. What do you think, doctor?"

There was a moment of complete silence. Blythe heard the doctor's fingernails drumming thoughtfully on his desk. Once or twice he asked a question which Mr. Hyland answered briefly. Then the silence closed in again.

"There are risks involved in everything we do," Dr. Harrison began, and Blythe's chest was too tight for breath, "and certainly permitting her to be the first to ride a mare that until a comparatively short time ago ran wild, would be a risk but as I understand it, her improvement dates from the time she first became interested in this horse. Right?"

Blythe could picture her father's nod of agreement in the short silence.

"The professional approach is, of course, much more impersonal than that of a parent, but any doctor can tell you that there is much more to this healing business than what is taught in medical schools. No matter what miracles of medicine may be accomplished, the patient must still have the will to live—or in this case, the will to do. That buckskin mare has been the incentive that has led her from one improvement to another. Take it away and it might undo all the progress she has made thus far. I'd say let her try it!"

Blythe could contain her exuberance no longer and, grabbing a crutch, she burst through the door. The three adults were more than startled by this explosion in their midst. Mr. and Mrs. Hyland tried to scold her by telling what happens to eavesdroppers, but the light that glowed in her face was not to be snuffed out, thereby proving Dr. Harrison's point.

"Mind now, young lady. You're to be extra careful about everything you do with that mare. Don't take a single chance with her," he insisted.

"I won't, Dr. Harrison. Honest. You don't realize how careful I am, but I just *know* that Sunny will behave all right."

The trip to town was of no further interest to Blythe, and she impatiently waited while the shopping and errands were checked off. Anything that came before the moment when she could first mount Dark Sunshine was classed as a nuisance—whether it was eating, sleeping, working or playing.

Mr. Hyland had decreed that he must at least be present and not until the following morning could he find the time. At his insistence Blythe and Dan went through Dark Sunshine's training routine with several extra minutes on the longe line. Their father was more and more astonished.

"Blythe, you're your granddad all over again. I wonder why I ever hesitated at all. Well, let's see how she'll act with you aboard."

Nowithstanding her conviction that the mare would behave like a lady, Blythe's heart thumped wildly now that the hard-fought-for moment was here. Dan untied the hackamore's lead rope from the saddle and, wrapping one end around his hand, he picked his sister up in his arms.

"Easy, Sunny. Whoa, girl," she chided gently as Dan set her lightly in the saddle.

Feeling Blythe's feet and legs along her sides, the one place the burlap jacket had missed, the mare flinched nervously but stood her ground. Blythe sat motionless, babbling a constant stream of reassurances and cajolery, while one hand stroked the shining neck and patted the sloping shoulder. Seconds passed without the mare moving a muscle, not even one of her backward-set ears. Mr. Hyland grew more and more nervous as a minute went by.

"Watch her, hon. She's apt to make one terrific leap any time now. Some green horses act that way."

Another minute passed and Blythe's tensed muscles demanded relief. She changed positions ever so slightly and this broke the mare's trance. Her neck crooked and her head came around so she could look up at her rider. Soft lips nuzzled Blythe's toe questioningly as if to ask, "What's next?"

The trio relaxed with muffled laughter at such an anticlimax and Blythe offered a piece of sugar that was promptly accepted. Dan tightened up the lead rope and stepped forward with the mare beside him as unconcerned as she had been with her former load, the only difference being an arch in her neck and a prance to her step as if proud that at last she carried her friend.

"See, no difference between my riding and a bag of sand. I told you she wouldn't make any trouble, Dad!"

"Don't be too foxy, Miss Big-Britches. Sometimes it takes once or twice for a horse to catch on to what's happening and then, Bang! You see stars."

"Not Sunny. She knows what's going on and is glad. And, oh, so am I!"

Succeeding sessions proved Blythe's point for not one misstep did Dark Sunshine make, her only dido being one little crowhop when the end of a latigo slipped loose and slapped her under the belly. The mare's evident pride in supplanting

Dick as Blythe's mount showed in every feature, every action, from the glowing brown eyes to the proud tail carriage, and the only thing prouder than Sunny was her rider.

The mare's reining commenced as soon as Blythe felt certain that all possibility of tantrums had passed and the lead line was abandoned. Instead of working on the mouth like a bridle, the hackamore's action came on the lower jawbone just above the lip from pressure of the bosal or knot. With the reins slack there was no contact between bosal and skin but tightening the reins stiffened the knot so that it rubbed against the jawbone and soon the horse learned that relaxing and flexing the neck protected that tender spot.

Blythe held one rein in each hand during the first lessons, the direct pull guiding the mare, the indirect rein pushing the same way. At the start Dark Sunshine was confused by this apparent contradiction but her rider was unfailingly gentle and patient and as one lesson followed another the buckskin began to understand. With that first step passed, progress was rapid yet never hurried.

Simultaneously with her reining lessons Dark Sunshine was being taught to stand for mounting, and that point won, Blythe went on to the very important next step, having the horse stand quietly beside a mounting block, in this case a box or rock. Like most horses, the mare persisted in swinging her rump away from the block and, rather than helping the girl to mount, it hindered. Blythe and Dan tried everything they could think of to prevent this pivoting but nothing was successful.

"Sunny, my girl, you've just got to learn this little item or I'll always have to have some strong arm handy to toss me up.

Now let's try it again," Blythe coaxed patiently one day when Dan was helping his father and she was on her own.

Again the hindquarters swung away in what seemed like an involuntary arc, for the horse was quiet and unafraid. Blythe ruffled her hair thoughtfully and looked around the corral for an inspiration, finding it in the fence.

"Here, girl. Come on over here."

Blythe dragged the box near the fence, leaving just enough room for the horse to walk between, and limped back for Sunny. Very slowly she led the buckskin into the narrow aisle and halted her. Then she scrambled up on the box and stood there talking to the mare, petting her and fussing with the saddle, the stirrups, the straps. To simulate weight in the stirrup she pulled down on the leather, tightening the reins when Dark Sunshine would have moved.

With the instincts of a true horseman Blythe chose the right moment for her move—when the mare understood that she must stand straight and quiet yet before the delay had made her nervous. The left foot found the stirrup and Blythe flashed into the saddle, her right leg swinging over the golden back with a freedom it had not known a few months earlier.

The reins checked a step forward and Blythe sat there quietly a moment. Then slowly and deliberately she swung her leg back and stepped down on the box.

"We've got it, Sunny. I think that's the ticket until you learn what's wanted."

Thereafter every session of girl and horse included several times on and off. By then Dark Sunshine was answering to the reins and Blythe concluded that they must graduate from the corral to outside work.

"Well, Dad, Sunny and I are ready to ride outside. Got any riding chores you need handled?" she asked at supper, her eyes twin stars.

"Nothing in particular, but Dan and I will be glad to have company tomorrow. It's high time that mare of yours makes friends with someone besides old Dick. Better under saddle than loose in the horse pasture too. We'll have to be careful for a while about which of 'em we turn out together."

Blythe could talk of nothing that night but her horse until even her easy-going family felt the strain.

"Amy, I'll tip you off," her father said for diversion. "You'd better be sure to get to bed first every night or sometime you'll find that mare right there in your bed."

"At least she wouldn't talk in her sleep like Amy does," Blythe retorted smartly, but at the same time she took the hint.

XIV: Shasta

WEEKS FLEW past like days for the happy girl, who was so absorbed in her companionship with Dark Sunshine that little else seemed real. Her mare proved able to look after herself when turned out with the other horses and though there was much running and kicking and squealing it was all in play. When the fun was over and siesta time arrived, however, it was always old Dick that Sunny turned nose to tail with for maximum fly protection.

From the first the buckskin came to Blythe's whistle like a homing pigeon and it was soon regular procedure for Mr. Hyland or Dan to let Sunny out of the horse pasture the first thing in the morning. She moseyed around the yard, nipping any tender grass shoots that might have sprung up around the water tank and snooping into any open doorway.

As soon as Blythe had completed her indoor chores for her mother, she had only to step out the back door and whistle to the mare who raced for Blythe's caress. A place for saddle and hackamore had been made on the porch and slipping one over the ears and buckling the other in place, the world was hers. If Dick had given her legs, Dark Sunshine had given her wings and her crutch leaning against the back of the house was mute evidence of her release from bondage.

Under Blythe's careful handling the mare progressed unbelievably fast, like a smart child that enters school late but makes up grades rapidly. Hours of careful walking gave her balance and a good response to the reins before she was ever speeded up. Her first canter for Blythe was more of a gallop and for a moment the girl gloried in their speed, the lightness of her horse, before she checked.

Dark Sunshine was so eager to please, Blythe had only to make her wishes understandable and they were as good as accomplished. At a collected canter Blythe began cutting easy circles, first one way, then the other. In the beginning the mare was pulled back to a trot from which to change leads but Blythe had so little love for that rough gait she concentrated on changing leads in stride and the willing horse obliged. At first she sometimes did it imperfectly and became disunited, but a more pronounced shift in weight, Blythe found, corrected the trouble and she was doubly proud for herself and her horse.

"Town tomorrow, kids. Everyone be ready to leave promptly—after the complete treatment," Mr. Hyland announced one night at supper.

"Guess I'll skip it, Dad. Sunny's coming along so well I don't want to miss a single day 'til I have to."

"That's means tomorrow, hon. Know what Monday is?"

Blythe had thought that declining the trip to town would settle her part and took a bite of meat, but her father's question stopped her in mid-bite. She chewed thoughtfully a moment.

"Monday, I guess, is all I can think of. It isn't your birth— no, of course, it isn't. Well, what is it then?"

"It's Labor Day and the day after that means school. Thought we'd stop in tomorrow and enroll the lot of you. Might as well take care of it in advance so you'll be all set when classes start next week."

Released early from the restrictions of a city school because of their move and turned out to ranch freedom, the summer had seemed endless to the happy Hylands, and their father's announcement was little short of a major catastrophe. It was a subdued quartet of young folks who scrubbed and combed and polished themselves for their trip to town.

Blythe could have wept at the thought of interrupting Dark Sunshine's education and for one wild second she debated trying to beg off because of her lameness, but saner reflection made her blush that she had even thought of it. The four young folks' cheerfulness was crushed at finding this blank wall at the end of their wonderful summer, but once the first shock was past and they accepted the unavoidable fact, little currents of curiosity about their teachers, their new classmates, their schools' activities showed them a door in the wall through which they were soon ready to pass.

The four Hylands would be scattered among three different schools, it developed—Amy going into second grade at one school, Chris entering junior high for his first year and Blythe and Dan in senior high, she a sophomore, he a junior. While almost a year older than Blythe, Dan's birthday had been a few days too late to start school ahead of his sister, and so they had entered together and progressed together—until her illness. Even then his coaching had helped her so much she had lost but one year.

Their credentials were presented at the superintendent of schools' office where it was Mr. Hyland's turn for a jolt. No school bus ran toward the Lazy SL! His brow furrowed with worry during the day's shopping and errands. The pick-up was too important on the ranch to be spared five full days a week, but somehow the children would have to get to school.

The final ritual of their trip to town, once every item had been checked off their list, was a stop at the soda fountain for the week's splurge. Blythe noticed that her father was too preoccupied to enjoy his ice cream and she felt a guilty twinge at the new clothes her mother had bought for her. She was accordingly unprepared for his startling statement.

"Mary, I don't see anything else to do but find a second-hand car for these kids to drive to school in. Think the bank balance can stand it?"

"Looks like it will have to, Ty. They certainly can't walk, and it's too far to ride horseback in all weather. It's funny I'd never connected the absence of other children for ours to play with with the fact that there mightn't be a school bus coming in our direction."

"All right, folks. Let's go down to the used car lot and have a look."

Dan and Chris were delirious with glee at the prospect of a car, but their ardor was somewhat dampened when they saw which ones their father was looking at. Final choice was between a battered jeep and an old sedan that had an air of decayed gentility.

"What do you think, son? Which gets your vote?"

Dan was briefly silent. He knew which was the better car but his hesitation came from wondering whether that good-looking girl he had met at the fountain would ever consent to ride in so beat-up a vehicle.

"The jeep, Dad," he finally answered like a man. "It's insides are in a lot better shape than its outsides. Besides, if we got a power take-off it would come in pretty handy around the ranch."

"Good. I like that one better too, and it may be you kids will need that four-wheel drive during bad weather. I've a notion the bottom could drop right out of that road after a wet spell."

The deal was soon concluded. Dan and Chris were to follow the pick-up back to the ranch, but the others had been home and unloaded for some time before the boys arrived.

"Had to drive around a little and show it off, I guess, eh, son?" Mrs. Hyland laughed tolerantly.

"Sort of, but mostly I was getting some sandpaper and paint. Thought I'd give it a face-lifting this week end—just to keep up appearances, you know."

Blythe heard this exchange and was no more fooled than her mother by Dan's airy explanation. The girl's loyalties were wrenched in many directions, one part of her wanting to spend the entire week end with Dark Sunshine but another telling her that here was a chance to help Dan when it counted. He had never disclosed the identity of the object of his admiration and this first secret between them made Blythe a little jealous, but if Dan needed help to fix up the car, he should have it!

"I'll help you sand it down, Dan. That's what takes the most time. Come on, we can get started while Mom's fixing supper."

Two short rides on Sunny while they were waiting for the paint to dry were all Blythe could manage but Dan's proud appraisal of the finished article was ample reward. What Dark Sunshine was to her, the jeep was to Dan and he fondled the steering wheel, the gear shift as lovingly as his sister would a dusky mane.

"We ought to give it a name," she suggested to help prolong his thrill. "Something short and neat—but clever."

"Maybe we should. What? Something like Shasta?"

"Why, 'cause she's a daisy?"

"Partly, but mostly because 'Shasta have gas and Shasta have oil'!"

"Perfect, Dan. Just perfect. Shall I break a bottle over your head to christen it?"

The four young Hylands glistened like new saddles when they were ready to leave on their first school day. Meeting new people and making new friends, a prospect that would have demoralized Blythe a few months earlier, served instead as a magnet and she was the first in the jeep.

"You look extra pretty this morning, dear. That shade of blue does something for your eyes."

Mrs. Hyland's first glance had been one of inspection, but

the crisp wave in her daughter's hair that had won back its gold lights, an even tan with an undercoat of real pink, and the sparkle in the clear blue eyes made her realize all over again what progress Blythe had made.

"Thanks, Mom, you do too." Blythe tweaked her mother's ear affectionately, half guessing at the intended encouragement. "Don't worry about me. I'll get along all right."

Blythe meant her brave words then, but when Dan had parked the jeep and Blythe had to get out and hobble up the front walk before scores of curious eyes, her courage ebbed. He sensed her lack of confidence and stayed with her until they had located her home room.

"Buck up, Butch. All isn't lost. I'll see you at noon."

She looked up gratefully, ready to accept his offer until she remembered that he too was new and had friends to make. She took a stronger grip on her new self-reliance.

"Thanks, Dan, but I'll be all right. I'll meet you at Shasta when classes are out."

School routine picked her up and carried her through its formalities of signing up for classes, issuing textbooks, assignment of lockers. At first all the girls were strangers but gradually one face would stand out, another's mannerism, and by the time the entire student body marched to the auditorium for assembly Blythe thought she knew which ones she would like to be friends with.

One vivacious redhead seemed somehow familiar and when she fell in beside Blythe the latter tried to clear up the mystery.

"Did you ever live in San Diego?"

"Goodness, no! I was born in Red Rock and have lived

here all my life. I don't think I could bear it in a big city where you can't ride and rope and have fun."

That did it, and Blythe's memory carried her back several months to her train trip to Red Rock, the cattle by the siding, the redheaded cowhand.

"Now I know. You live on a ranch and ride a blaze-faced sorrel!"

The girl looked at her in surprise, as if to see whether a crystal ball was concealed in a pocket.

"No, I live right here in town, but I do ride—and own—a blaze-faced sorrel. How'd you know?"

Blythe quickly recounted their first meeting, if it could be called that, and before they were seated in the auditorium they had laid the foundations of a lasting friendship.

"My name's Maggie Ramsey," the other whispered as the principal rapped for order.

"Mine's Blythe Hyland."

Assembly opened with several songs and Maggie rolled her eyes appreciatively at Blythe's silvery soprano. When, after a series of routine announcements, the principal stated that glee club try-outs would be held that afternoon, Maggie nudged her significantly. Blythe's spirits soared at finding there was something she could join in, for she would never be content to be just a passenger through school. She wanted to do her share toward making the school something besides a building.

"I won't need legs for glee club," she thought happily. "I hope Dan won't mind waiting for me. Maybe he could go and pick up Chris and Amy first."

She had a jauntier air when she limped out of the auditorium. Occasionally she caught glimpses of Dan in the halls as classes passed and he always seemed to be part of a happy-go-lucky crowd. When Blythe stopped to explain that she would be late meeting him, she introduced Maggie and Dan, hoping her new friend was the girl he so admired, but her hopes were dashed when they met like strangers.

"Did you warble loud enough to satisfy 'em?" he greeted her after school.

"I think so. Won't know for sure 'til tomorrow when names are posted."

A shadow darkened her eyes for an instant and Dan misread it as uncertainty.

"How'd things go with you, small fry?" He directed his question at the boy and girl in the rear bucket seats.

"Just fine, Dan," Amy chirped. "We drew pictures and teacher picked mine for one to hang up in front."

"What about you, Chris? Why so strangely silent?"

"What do you want me to do, cheer?"

"What desk were you assigned?"

"One in the front row."

"Is that the one you picked out when you first went in?"

"Nope."

"Where was that one?" Big brother's cross examination continued.

"Back row."

"Um-huh! Sounds like you've already been in trouble." Dan could read between the lines of even such monosyllables as his bumptious young brother's.

Barren though its surroundings might be, the Lazy SL had the welcoming look of home to the quartet. As though it was a race, they scattered to change their clothes. Blythe had already spotted Dark Sunshine loitering near the barn and it was but a matter of minutes before the girl re-entered the kitchen wearing her jeans and boots.

"How soon is supper, Mom? Have I got time for a ride?"

"Yes, a short one. Thought you might be pining for one so I started things a little late." Mrs. Hyland's unerring mother instincts had guided her right.

Supper-table talk was a rapid-fire review of the four's day and when Amy wasn't trying to describe every child in her grade, Dan or Blythe was raving about their beautiful school and grounds—"Most like a college campus," they agreed—or Chris was muttering darkly about "that teacher."

Everyone was interested in Blythe's account of her try-out for glee club which, like a continued story, would not be finished until the next night.

"I'm pretty sure I'll make it though. The director said I had a very nice voice."

Conversation flowed on around her but Blythe was silent, remembering the actual conversation which she could never tell her folks. She knew what a struggle lay ahead of them on the Lazy SL as well as they did, and there was no use making them feel bad. Better to keep the director's praise to herself and her voice for family festivities. Still his words echoed through her head.

"You have a really remarkable voice, Miss Hyland. Its purity of tone, its depth and power are most unusual in an untrained voice. It is untrained, of course?"

His words were both statement and question. Blythe nodded.

"I'd like to see you have some training. Not here in school —we haven't the time for individual work nor the personnel—

but there happens to be a fine teacher living here now—expensive, of course. Would you be interested in talking with him?"

"No, I'm sorry. It's out of the question. I'll just have to sing for the fun of it."

"It's a pity. I'm curious as to what built up such power. Any idea?"

"Not unless it was all the outdoor singing I've done to my horse. She likes it."

"I should think she would. It's casting pearls before horses," he paraphrased whimsically.

XV: Like a Cripple

FIVE HYLANDS rejoiced with Blythe the following evening when she told them that not only had she made the glee club but she was to be included in its triple trio. Mrs. Hyland hurriedly added a white frosting with a clef of red candies to the cake she had baked for supper and the meal was a triumphant one for the girl.

"What does the glee club do besides sing for its own amusement, hon?" her father queried.

"Oh, we sing at assemblies and parties and sometimes at some of the town's special functions, like Christmas. There're a lot of places where a group of good singers comes in handy."

"And you're pretty sure you'll be good?"

"Absolutely! Our music teacher is one of the best in the

state. A few years ago the glee club won a cup in a state-wide competition. Convinced?"

"Convinced. All this musical talk makes me feel like bursting into song. Why don't we have a Hyland hoe-down tonight? Feel like pumping your squeeze-box a while, Blythe?"

"That I do. I'm ready to burst into song any minute. Mi, mi, mi, mi, mi," she caroled an ascending scale and somehow even that sounded good.

Their songfest sounded still better and Blythe's accordion led them from one song to another. At their children's insistence Mr. and Mrs. Hyland sang a duet which easily explained why Blythe had a fine voice and the others had good ones. Amy and Chris obliged with a joint rendition of "Lavender's Blue, Dilly, Dilly," making it Blythe's and Dan's turn but she begged off.

"I'm all sung out." Her fingers roved restlessly over the accordion's keyboard. "Forgot to tell you folks I joined the girls' riding club today."

"Didn't know they had one. What do they do, sugar?" Her mother pricked up her ears at further proof of her daughter's return to normal yet sensed that something was amiss.

"Perform for assemblies, of course, Mary," her husband retorted facetiously. "Just like the glee club does."

"Just ride for fun—trail rides and such," Blythe corrected loftily. "Once a year they have a gymkhana, and members are encouraged to participate in all community riding events."

"Is it a nice group of girls, Blythe?" her mother persisted. "Do you like them?"

"All but one, the one I talked to about joining."

"Wasn't she nice to you?"

"Oh, yes, she was terribly nice—and I do mean terribly—but she treated me like a cripple! She was sweet, just sicky sweet, and said they ride pretty hard and wouldn't I rather be an 'honorary member.'"

"Who was it, Butch? I hope you let her have both barrels." Even Dan had not heard this chapter and anger rose in his face and voice.

"No, I was terribly sweet too, and told Rhoda that if they decided I couldn't ride as hard and as fast as the others I'd resign."

"Rhoda! Why, she isn't like that!" Aggrieved surprise struggled with indignation when Dan learned the identity of his sister's detractor.

"Maybe not—if you're tall and handsome—and a boy." In a flash she understood that Rhoda was Dan's dream girl and Blythe tried to soft-pedal her animosity. "She was really quite nice after Maggie explained that I owned a horse and rode a lot."

"Then they did let you in?" Mrs. Hyland followed up.

"Yes, but I'd better be good when they have their first ride."

"Don't worry, hon. You will be, but all this talk of glee clubs and riding clubs and such makes me curious." Mr. Hyland introduced a lighter note. "You kids do manage to attend a class now and then, don't you?"

"I'll say we do, Dad, and that reminds me—I still have some history reading to do for tomorrow." Blythe punctuated her exclamation with a crash as she let the air out of her accordion.

The short week was soon ended and Blythe had two full days to spend with Dark Sunshine, but it was Monday morning before Blythe had done half the things that she wanted to. Then it was Shasta's turn to give her a ride to school. Several blocks from school they overtook Maggie, walking, and gave her a lift.

"We have to drive right past your house, Maggie. Why don't you wait there and we'll honk for you. Might as well save all that energy of yours for more important things," Blythe suggested.

"Go on. Coax me. All right, I will and thanks a lot," her new friend rattled on. "Say, I hear there are big things cooking today."

"Like for instance?" Dan wanted to know.

"Did you ever hear of Marilyn Forbes?"

"Sort of. Wasn't she the girl who was killed last year in an auto accident?"

"Yes. She was a wonderful girl, just all around tops with practically a straight A average, class officer, on the school paper and a swell athlete—but pretty and popular too. She was an only child, and at first it nearly killed her father and mother too, but Daddy says they're getting ahold of themselves now. I hear that there's to be an announcement at assembly about a memorial."

"What kind of a memorial?" Blythe asked when Maggie paused for breath.

"That I don't know. Might be any one of several things."

"That must be why the glee club has been rehearsing such solemn songs this week."

"We'll soon know," Dan said, wheeling the jeep into a parking space.

During the classes that intervened Blythe had no time to think of Maggie's words and when the bell rang for assembly

she hurried as fast as she was able to join the glee club backstage. Stairs were the most difficult thing for Blythe to manage and she was grateful for the sheltering door at the foot
of the steps.

Singing was as easy and natural to Blythe as to a bird sitting in a tree and the added joy of blending her voice with
others made her forget all else, even leaning on her crutch
before several hundred people. Their two selections completed, the glee club took the seats arranged for them on the
platform and the principal rose, but it was not his words she
heard. Instead those of the music director rang in her ears like
a knell.

If only her family could afford singing lessons for her—but
she knew it was impossible. Even had there happened to be
any extra money it would not be fair to the others to use it
all on her. If only she could earn some money of her own!
But where could she get any kind of a job let alone one that
would pay enough for an expensive teacher? If only—

"And so I have been authorized by Mr. and Mrs. Lester
Forbes to announce the Marilyn Forbes Memorial Scholarship," the principal's words broke in on Blythe's milling
thoughts. "It shall be open to any tenth or eleventh grade
girl on the basis of scholarship and all around achievement
both in the field of athletics and other school activities. The
personality of the applicants will also be considered as it is
the purpose of this award to help in the development of a
school leader who in time will become a community leader,
a real asset to society.

"So far as actual monetary value is concerned there is no
set limit, the idea being to handle all expenses incurred in car-

rying out the purpose of the scholarship. Details are available with the faculty counselors and any girl who wishes to be considered a candidate should discuss it first with her counselor who will make an appointment for her with the committee of which Mr. and Mrs. Forbes are members."

Whatever routine announcements Mr. Jackson may have made after that were lost on Blythe to whom the scholarship loomed like the answer to a prayer. She feverishly reviewed her qualifications. Scholarship? yes. It was already good and could be better with closer application. Extra-curricular activities? ye-e-s. Glee club membership should be a big factor and there were other things she could go out for. Athletics? no! Blythe's dreams crashed to bits when she faced this requirement and by no twist of her imagination could she make it seem possible.

"I'd look like a ninny even going out for basketball or baseball or hockey. I'd make a joke of my whole application."

Her disappointment was so keen she felt tears of frustration behind her eyelids. Whatever resentment she may have felt previously over her handicap was mild compared to the bitterness that boiled up within her now. Blythe was not made of quitter stuff, however, and the next instant she resolved to try.

"I'll go out for the baseball team anyway. Monte Stratton didn't have any leg at all!"

Blythe was not a fool and the next instant she realized that there the similarity ceased. After all, Monte Stratton had already made a place for himself on the team before his accident.

"Come on, what're you waiting for?" The voice of the

soprano next to her jarred Blythe back to reality and the end of assembly.

She scrambled to her feet, feeling like a convict with a ball and chain on her right leg. Lunch hour and the afternoon passed with little help from Blythe. When classes ended for the day Dan stopped her to say that he would be a few minutes late.

"I'll go and talk it over with Miss Davis. She's nice and maybe can think of something for me to do," Blythe decided. "I'll not be satisfied until I've done something about it."

Miss Davis was tidying up her desk before going home, but she looked up at the thump of Blythe's crutch in the doorway. The girl stood tongue-tied, already discomfited by her daring.

"Hello there, Blythe. Come in. What can I do for you?"

"Well, I—can you—what about the scholarship?" she finally blurted.

The teacher looked at the slender girl leaning on her crutch, just the toe of her right foot touching the floor, longing and hope and misery shining in her eyes. Miss Davis's fingers itched to draw a heavy black line through the words "athletic ability" and not being able to made her especially gentle.

"Come in, Blythe. The committee has mimeographed a sheet that gives all the information. Do you have time to read one now? Then we can talk it over."

Blythe nodded and greedily read the details.

"Winner to be announced at Commencement the end of May . . . outstanding personality . . . maturity of viewpoint . . . committee to weigh candidates' achievements carefully and pick recipient in consultation with Mr. and Mrs.

Forbes . . . scholarship . . . leadership . . . athletic ability
. . . 'a sound mind in a sound body.' "

A hot blush of embarrassment stained her neck and face.
Mumbling a hasty "thank you" she hurried to the door only
to remember the paper she still held in her hand. All she
wanted was to get out, and she feverishly sought a place to
drop it.

"That's for you to keep if you'd like, Blythe. Take it home
and then come and see me tomorrow."

Dan found Blythe hunched up in the jeep. Her eyes looked
enormous in her pinched face, and for an instant he thought
she was ill. Then the crumpled paper in her fist explained
more quickly to him than words what had happened.

"Don't mind, Sis. Everybody can't win it."

"But, Dan, think how wonderful it would be. Not only
would it save Dad all the expense for my schooling but I'd
have things that I couldn't ever hope for otherwise."

"Take it easy. What, for instance? Dad's looking after
us mighty well, I think."

"He is—of course, he is, but if I could win the scholarship
I could have singing lessons."

At last Blythe broke her restraint and told Dan of the
music teacher's words, that he thought she had the most prom-
ising voice he'd ever heard but that it needed training.

"For lack of a leg, the voice was lost," she ended bitterly
when they stopped for the younger children.

XVI: Merry-go-round

"All we have to do, Butch, is figure out some sort of athletics you can do. Swimming, for instance." As though there had been no interruption, Dan picked up the thread of their conversation the next morning as soon as Amy and Chris had jumped out in front of their schools and been swallowed by the hordes of youngsters.

"No go there, Dan. Marilyn was a champion swimmer and it would look as though I was trying to imitate her. A swimmer needs the drive of two good legs anyway, if she's to get there first—and I'm afraid I've been a dry-land girl too long."

"Archery then?"

"They don't 'arch' here."

Blythe fell silent, reviewing all the wild ideas she had had
for qualifying. On reaching home the day before she had
saddled Dark Sunshine and gone for a ride, the carefully
smoothed out sheet of requirements in her hip pocket, and
away in the privacy of the open range she had taken it out
and reread it, but it still added up the same.

"If only you could handle the athletics for me, Sunny,"
she murmured, caressing the strong shoulder. "Without your
legs I'm just no good."

She snapped back to her immediate surroundings.

"No, Dan, there's just no hope. If I could play baseball on
horseback—it's too bad they don't have a polo team. I might
be able to do something there."

"That's a lead, Butch. You belong to their riding club.
Make them sit up and take notice. That's the ticket."

"It would be a start, but mostly it's just rides and stuff. The
only competitive thing is their gymkhana."

"You said they encourage participation in the interscholastic
rodeo, so enter other ones too. That ought to show 'em."

"Winning a rodeo event now and then—if I could, which I
doubt, as Sunny and I aren't up to it yet—wouldn't be outstanding enough. If I could just think of something big, something super, that anyone would be proud to do."

So intent were they with Blythe's problem the jeep had
nearly passed Maggie before they recognized her hail and
picked her up, full of chatter and news. She rattled on gaily,
her conversation as good as a newspaper for catching up on
school news and personalities, and the two Hylands were content to listen until Dan slipped in a question during a short
pause.

"What's the most important horsey event of the year in Red Rock, Maggie?"

"The endurance ride, of course!" Her answer bounced back quick as a ping-pong ball.

"Endurance ride? Never heard of it. What's it like?"

"You never heard of it! Why, it's held the latter part of every May and riders come from miles around to enter it. That dark fellow in your class who drives the cut-down Ford came in second last year."

"Oh, it's open to everybody, young and old, eh?"

"It sure is, and some of the old folks have to keep on their toes to beat the young fry. Year before last I rode part way just for fun."

"Think I'll stay here in Shasta and review my English a little," Blythe murmured when they stopped in front of the high school. "Bell won't ring for a few minutes yet."

"Me, too," Dan agreed, but Maggie jumped out, intent on her own pursuits.

"That's the ticket for you, Butch! Boy, if you could win that endurance ride it'd show 'em you're no chintz."

"Do you think I could? Do you think Sunny could? She's as important as I am."

"Of course she could. She's a strong, young mare and with proper conditioning she could do it in a breeze. Both Morgans and Arabians are noted for their stamina."

"It certainly sounds like the best bet yet. I wonder . . ."

"You don't need to. Uncle Dan has spoken. You skip in to your adviser again and sign up, and don't give me any back talk! Come on, we'd better get going."

Throughout the day Blythe argued the pros and cons with

herself, or tried to think she was, when all the time she was waiting for her vacant sixth period so she could go back to talk with Miss Davis. The figure that limped into the teacher's office looked the same, though there was a difference that was immediately felt. Where there had been doubt and uncertainty the day before there was determination and confidence. This seemed to make her seem taller and straighter, even stronger.

"I'd like to sign up as a candidate for the Memorial Scholarship, Miss Davis. Is there anything else that I ought to do?"

"Let's talk it over a little. What are your extra interests and how good were your grades in junior high, for instance?"

Miss Davis started with the obvious, hoping that Blythe would go on to the next consideration, and she did with a disarming matter-of-factness.

"As for the athletic qualification, Miss Davis, mine will have to be with my horse as a second member of my team. The only good legs I have are hers, but on horseback I can meet the others as equals. I'd rather not tell you just exactly what as you'd probably think I'm silly but I'm sure it will work out all right. What else must I do now?"

"Next Monday you will have to meet with the committee, but aside from that all you need to do is pitch in. And I'll certainly be pulling for you."

With the new peace of mind she had achieved once her course of action was determined, Blythe was able to tell her mother and father that night of the wonderful opportunity that had come to the girls of Red Rock High. Dan served as an alternate when she had to stop to eat or breathe and the Hylands soon knew almost as much about it as the candidate

herself. Almost, for Blythe found it difficult to use the words
"endurance ride" in connection with herself, and the phrase
"competitive long distance trail ride" was entirely too high-
sounding. Time enough later when it was closer, she told herself.

"That's quite a hunk of work you're biting off for yourself, dear, but if you can win the scholarship it will be more
than worth it. It's too bad you have to do it during school—
but if that weren't so the opportunity wouldn't be there."
Mrs. Hyland hastily corrected herself before anyone else
could. "Looks like I had better not count on you for much
help this year."

"I was hoping you'd see the light, Mom. It is going to take
just about all the time I can squeeze out of twenty-four hours
a day—and sometimes if I have to stay for a meeting or something all of us may be late getting home. Mind?"

"No, dear. You can't make an omelet without breaking
eggs. We'll manage—starting now. Don't bother with the
dishes. Amy's getting to be such a big girl she can help. Better get to your books."

Monday morning Blythe dressed with infinite care for her
appointment with the selection committee. She felt so clean
she was sure she must squeak as she walked, yet she was no
more spotless than the other girls she found waiting in the
principal's outer office. A casual observer might have judged
from their expressions they were dressed up for their own
funerals.

Interviews were going forward on an alphabetical basis,
so Blythe had ample time to size up her competition and it
was not reassuring. Such hearty, healthy girls she thought

she had never seen, nor were they exclusively robust, for Blythe could read character well enough to tell that their minds were equally vigorous. "A sound mind in a sound body" rang in her ears momentarily but she resolutely turned her attention to counting those present.

At first the large number of candidates worried her. They stretched all along one side of the office and Blythe wondered how many might have already come and gone, but her innate good sense came to her rescue.

"After all, if there were only two of us, I wouldn't win unless I was good enough, so what does it matter how many others there are?"

Interviews moved along to Garber, Gunther, Hayes, Holman.

"Blythe Hyland, please."

Of all times Blythe's crutch slipped to the floor with a crash, making her face extra pink when she rose and walked haltingly into the committee room. A blur of faces watched her enter and seat herself, but they gradually assumed form and personality. Miss Davis she recognized first, then the principal and one or two other teachers. Blythe decided that the man and woman at the far end of the table were Mr. and Mrs. Forbes, though there was time for only a fleeting impression.

Evidently Miss Davis had briefed the committee with such information as she had on Blythe's background and plans, the one gap being the athletic achievement she would undertake. This the principal, as spokesman, arrived at soon.

"Miss Davis tells us that you are a member of the school's

riding club and that you intend to qualify for Point Three through that."

"Yes, sir." Blythe's answer was forthright enough but the principal had hoped that it would be more explicit. He thoughtfully rolled his pencil between finger and thumb.

"I'm afraid that mere membership would not be considered sufficient, Miss Hyland."

"Oh, I intend to do more than just the club meetings and its gymkhana."

"What exactly did you have in mind?"

"We-ll, would winning the endurance ride be enough?"

Blythe misinterpreted the startled silence that followed her question, as each member contrasted her halting entrance with her brave words.

"I understand that that's the outstanding horseback event of the year here. Wouldn't winning it be satisfactory?"

"Yes, Miss Hyland, it certainly would, but suppose you couldn't—or didn't—finish? That would be something else again."

"Oh, I'm not worried about that. My Sunny's a dandy. She won't have any trouble."

In the face of such unself-consciousness not one committee member dared raise the question of Sunny's rider, and Blythe's interview was soon at an end, her application approved.

From that moment forward Blythe felt that she had stepped onto a merry-go-round and while part of it was fun, much of it was just plain hard work. Her studies, she found, were the hardest, for in the time she had been out of school she had lost the knack of studying, of getting things easily, as well as many facts which she had to review.

She always kept a textbook near her to insure that no minute would be wasted. She studied during her vacant periods,
of course, but also in the jeep, before supper, after supper and
many hours on Saturdays and Sundays. Eventually the work
became progressively easier and she was encouraged by the
higher marks she found on her papers.

Dark Sunshine had been almost ignored during Blythe's
feverish preoccupation with books and it was not until her
mother and father put their foot down that she resumed her
daily rides after school.

"There's no use making yourself sick all over again. You
need the outdoor exercise and Sunny needs riding if she's to
be fit for your riding club events. I don't think you'll miss
that hour much. In fact, your mind will be keener for a little
fresh air."

These afternoon rides were like a stimulating drink to
Blythe, who sometimes rode with the wind as Dark Sunshine's
hoofs pounded out a strong, triumphant rhythm. At other
times the two dawdled across the plain easily, the girl taking
strength and courage from the grandeur about her, strength
that she really needed for school activities.

Almost overnight Blythe had become a class favorite, and
her cheerful, friendly nature expanded under the warmth of
her classmates' regard. In a way her lameness was an asset,
not because of any sympathy it elicited, for she had won her
fight to be accepted on equal terms with the others, but it
made her stand out from the crowd just as a lot of freckles
or some other distinguishing feature would.

Maggie and Dan had constituted themselves a Committee
of Two on behalf of Blythe and when class elections were

announced Maggie went into action like a born politician. As a result there was a prompt second to her nomination of Blythe as sophomore vice-president and she was elected by a landslide.

"But what do I have to do? I've never been a class officer before," she protested wonderingly.

"Nothing! That's the beauty of being vice-president. All you have to do is look important—unless something should happen to Jerry Kennedy, the president. Then you'd have to take over," Maggie prattled happily.

"Goodness, I wouldn't want to do that. I hope nothing happens to him."

Blythe glanced quickly at the black-haired, blue-eyed president who had so easily assumed the mantle of class leadership, masking her admiration behind an unwillingness to pinch-hit with the gavel.

XVII: Whodunit!

BLYTHE FOUND the autumn weeks and months flipping past faster than the notes and bars of the songs she sang with the glee club, until she was practicing Christmas carols with them. To her great delight she was assigned a solo, *Joy to the World,* and no song could have better expressed her mood.

Only one thing troubled her and that was how to finance the extra grain that Dark Sunshine would need during her preparatory training. Blythe realized that if she was to earn any extra money for it, it must be during Christmas holidays, the only long vacation that intervened, but her scope was so limited she scarcely knew where to start. The answer came looking for her at the school's Christmas concert and dance.

The entire Hyland clan was there to hear Blythe in her first public solo, and the audience's reaction was no less enthusiastic than her family's. Going backstage after the concert, they found a radiant Blythe the center of an admiring crowd of schoolmates and friends, but one dapper man they couldn't place.

"Mom! Dad! What do you think? Mr. Tucker wants me to sing with the hotel's dining room ensemble during Christmas week. For pay! Imagine being paid to sing!"

At that Mr. Tucker introduced himself and explained more fully, but no matter what he said, Mr. and Mrs. Hyland were not in favor of it. Blythe took them off in a corner and hastily explained her need of the extra money, wishing she had done so earlier under less pressure, but they were adamant.

"How would you get back and forth to town, Blythe?"

"Oh, I could stay with Maggie. She's been coaxing me to come and visit her."

"No, dear. That would be too great a drain on your energies. You'll need all the pep you can muster if you enter—"

"Sh-h, Mom. Not so loud!"

"My goodness, Blythe, Gabriel himself couldn't be heard over the clatter of those chairs," Mrs. Hyland exclaimed above the noise made by a squad of vigorous boys who were folding chairs and pushing them out of the way to make ready for the dance.

"Sunny's going to need stacks and stacks of hay and grain to get in condition. How'll I ever get it?" Blythe worried.

"I guess I can still buy the feed our horses need," her father said shortly. "You invite Maggie out to visit us on the ranch."

"Yes, dear. If you weren't around it would spoil our first Christmas here."

"That's another thing. I'd have more money to buy presents with," Blythe wailed.

"That would only upset things more. We've agreed on small, homemade presents. Remember? Besides, you'll need the time for riding Sunny and keeping her in shape or she'll get fat and soft and logy. You wouldn't want that."

"No-o, that'd be awful—but it'd be such fun to sing in public."

"Don't worry, hon. With as nice a voice as you have, there'll be plenty of other chances," her father consoled, little realizing how close to the truth he was.

Mr. Hyland's approving words were lost on Blythe who had spotted a dark head approaching through the crowd. She hurriedly slipped an arm in her coat sleeve and was pulling it around her when Jerry Kennedy spoke to her.

"Hey, there. What for the coat? I thought you said you'd be staying for the dance."

"Don't be silly! Wouldn't I cut a fine figure on the dance floor?"

"But you said—"

"Of course, I did, but I was joking. Can't you take a joke?" Blythe snapped, mad at herself and therefore at Jerry. "Are you ready to go, Mom?"

Just as if she hadn't heard the exchange, Mrs. Hyland turned to her daughter who looked like a sassy kitten rebuffing a big dog's invitation to play.

"Ready to go? I should say not. Ty and I want to do some dancing first. Your arm, Mr. Hyland."

Their parents' sudden departure left the four young Hylands on their own. Dan hurried off in search of Rhoda, and

Chris and Amy joined the small fry who were milling around the auditorium. Blythe looked about irresolutely, then at Jerry who waited beside her, and the angry glints faded from her eyes.

"I don't know how to dance, Jerry, and couldn't if I did. You ought to know that."

"Mind if I sit it out with you then? I'm not feeling so frisky tonight." He stretched wearily. "How'd you make out with that English Lit exam yesterday?"

One topic led into another and they were talking so busily it excited the curiosity of several classmates who stopped by, and no matter what the dance tune there was always a knot of animated young folks around them. Jerry put an arm under Blythe's elbow.

"There's a waltz. Come on. Let's try it," he urged.

"No, I just can't dance. Don't you ever take 'no' for an answer?"

"Not unless I want to, and I don't want to. Come on, it'd be a cinch."

"No. N-o," she spelled, only to soften it with a smile. "No, thank you, of course."

After the waltz Mr. and Mrs. Hyland called it enough and began rounding up the others. Blythe found that in spite of her inaction she was reluctant to leave although she had Jerry's parting words to warm her on the dark ride home.

"Don't forget. I never take 'no' for an answer."

The party put everyone in an extra gay mood, and Christmas in their new home was as warm and happy a time as any of them could remember. Small though the presents were, they represented the best thought and efforts of their donors and were accordingly dear to the recipients.

Chris and Dan had outdone themselves on their present to the family. They had assembled a battery radio set during their shop work at school, so the house rang with music of all kinds. Blythe had taken advantage of school instruction to make leather wallets for the entire family except Amy, for whom she made a tiny handbag.

Blythe was in transports of delight over the radio which made it possible to hear so much music, but she also hovered lovingly over her other presents. Her mother had made a fancy saddle blanket to soften the saddle for Sunny, while her father had given her a sheepskin cover to soften the saddle for her. Amy had embroidered several rub rags with Blythe's initials.

"Thanks a lot, Amy, they're beautiful—so beautiful I'm going to save them for the endurance ride so I can show 'em off better. They'll be my good luck charms."

The spirit of Christmas still pervaded the old ranch house when Maggie came for her visit, and her merriment prolonged their festivities still more. She slipped into the particular niche that only Maggie could fill, teasing Chris, admiring and talking to Amy's doll family like people, and readily falling in with Dan's and Blythe's schemes.

The threesome scouted the range from one corner of the Lazy SL to the other, working toward the climax of a trip to the Pocket so Maggie could see where Blythe had found her dream horse. Not having to worry about midsummer heat, a midmorning start was planned, and they were at the corrals saddling up in a leisurely fashion when a car entered the drive.

"Shades of Apollo! It's Jerry," Blythe whispered. "Hello. Imagine meeting you here," she called to him.

"Hi. Just happened to be driving by so I thought I'd stop in."

"Glad you did, Kennedy. I need some help to keep these gals in line," Dan said cordially. "We're all set for a ride. Come along, why don't you?"

" 'Just happened to be driving by' indeed, Jerry Kennedy. Who else were you planning to visit up the road, Mr. and Mrs. Coyote?" Maggie jibed wickedly.

"Sa-ay, that buckskin mare of yours is a beauty, Blythe. Where'd you get her?" Jerry loftily ignored Maggie's sally.

"That's where we're going now. I'll tell you on the way."

Maggie's saddle was changed to Dick so that Jerry could ride the larger horse and the quartet set out. Blythe recounted the full story of finding the mare and reclaiming her, and Jerry was so full of admiration for Dark Sunshine, Blythe was moved to confide her hopes of winning the endurance ride with her.

"Good girl!" Jerry applauded. "You'll do it too or I miss my guess. She'll be perfect for it, steady, sound, game, good breeding and the straightest action I've seen in a horse. How's her trot?"

"Good, but we don't trot much. It shakes my eye teeth."

"Can't you post it, or are you too much a daughter of the West to post a trot?"

"I guess I just haven't tried since the first time before I had my 'sea legs.' She has a fast walk and wonderful canter, so we've skipped the trot."

"Let's see you try it. A trot is pretty important in making time on a long ride. Takes less out of your horse too. Look, I'll shorten your right stirrup a little more so you'll have equal weight in it. There, now see how it goes," he said, remounting.

Blythe bounced around at first but she soon caught the rhythm and found it comparatively easy. By adjusting the stirrup her right leg, though shorter, still bore some of her weight so that the exercise was something like walking without a crutch.

"That's not half bad. I bet it'll do more to improve my leg muscles than a year of walking would," she exclaimed, twin stars in her eyes.

Maggie and Dan had pulled up to find out what the delay was about and four abreast they rode across the level plain with short detours around greasewood and mesquite. Reaching the upward trail they strung out single file until they drew rein at the top of the Pocket. The horses pricked up their ears when Dick whinnied soulfully to the empty Pocket.

"Silly. Your girl friend is right here beside you now instead of down there," Blythe chuckled, only to redouble her laughter when Dark Sunshine too joined the equine chorus.

Vacation seemed over when Maggie elected to ride back to town with Jerry that night in order to save her father a special trip the next day. During the day or two that remained Blythe divided her time between her horse and her books and felt well repaid by her progress. Once tried, the trot was no longer so troublesome and she made herself post a few minutes more each day.

Her greatest triumph was in geometry, however. Throughout the fall it had been her most difficult subject and finally in desperation she had fallen back on memorizing the lessons. She knew that was not the way geometry should be done, that it was a matter of reasoning and logic, but she had decided that rather than jeopardize her scholarship standing she would learn the theorems by heart.

On the last day of vacation, New Year's Day in fact, Dan found her staring into space while reciting the next day's lesson, and he was horrified, even after her lame explanation. He puzzled a moment in silence. How to make it come alive for her? Sired by his own aptitude and out of a determination that Blythe should get a good mark, an inspiration was born.

"Here, Sis, pretend it's a 'Whodunit.' The theorem is a crime—"

"I'll say it is, the way I do it!"

"Please, please! Let's keep our mind on our work. The theorem is the scene of a crime and all the axioms and corrolaries are clues by which you are to solve it. If this is true and that is true, it proves that something else is equal to something else and there you are. QED!" he finished triumphantly.

"You make it seem so easy, Dr. Anthony," Blythe murmured, "but maybe it's worth a try. Let's see now."

She picked up her pencil and stumbled through the next day's lesson with occasional prompting from Dan, and she was so encouraged she would have turned back to the preceding theorem but he went her one better and flipped back to the front of the book.

"Might as well do the thing right and start at the beginning," he decreed.

By bedtime Blythe felt that for the first time she grasped

the principles underlying the science of geometry and she was impatient to get to school to try her new approach. The day was dark and cold with a raw north wind that made the four Hylands grateful for the top and side curtains on the jeep.

"Br-r-r, it smells like snow." Blythe sniffed the air judiciously. "It sure does."

"Snow, Blythe? Does it really snow down here," Chris asked.

"That it does, and a good thing. It means just that much more moisture for the grass, and we can use every bit we get. I hope it does."

"Me too," Amy seconded. "I've never seen any."

Blythe's weather prophecy was fulfilled that afternoon when they were driving home, and the youngsters were beside themselves with delight. During a succession of damp, raw days they saw more of it, but other than a few snowballs and a stunted snowman there was never enough to really have fun in. In fact, before the month was out they had tired of the mud and the cold and when the sun shone again they were glad to see the end of their short winter. The weather stayed cold, but so long as the sky was blue and the sun bright, the mud underfoot was unimportant with trusty Shasta to pull them through.

Taking her cue from the weather that seemed to conspire to help her, Blythe focused all her attention on her school work, for that was the month of final examinations. She felt a justifiable pride when her report card showed only A's, even though several other scholarship candidates had done equally well.

Her Committee of Two, Maggie and Dan, looked very grave over the situation and immediately convened in a parley. Blythe was tempted to giggle at their solemn demeanor, but remembering how much she wanted to win restored her own solemnity.

"Blythe, the only thing for you to do this semester is not to be satisfied with measly little old A's. You step out and get yourself some A pluses."

"As easy as that, eh? Just a few A pluses," Blythe echoed sarcastically. "How would you suggest that I go about it?"

"Well, once in a great while in geometry, for instance"— Dan used his specialty as an example—"there're two ways to arrive at the same solution. When you've got it down pat one way, keep fiddling around to see whether you can find another route to the same goal. That would surprise and please the old boy, but good. I'll help you, of course," he added hastily by way of smothering the fire in his sister's eye.

"And in your other subjects, don't be content to have just the right answer, Blythe," Maggie suggested, "but sharpen up on its backgrounds, the hows and whys, correlate what you're doing in Lit with what's happening in history—and then serve it all up with a conciseness that'll make 'em blink!"

Their proposal simmered in the back of Blythe's mind a day or two until she concluded she must try it or risk failure. It would entail a supreme effort but the prize was worth her best and she determined to make her marks not just outstanding but unique in the purest sense of the word—single in kind or excellence, unequaled.

XVIII: Added Attractions

ABOUT THAT grain you said you'd buy for Sunny, Dad. I guess the time has come. I'm going to put her in training tomorrow."

It was the middle of February and Blythe could begin to see daylight through her welter of book work, the ground had dried out enough to provide good footing, and she wanted to start Sunny in ample time to insure a slow, careful conditioning.

"Of course, right at first she won't need much extra feed until the work gets harder."

"Are you sure you want to do it, hon? I've been talking with folks around town and it sounds like quite an order."

"Am I sure! Why, Dad, my whole year's work will be

wasted if I don't do it. Sunny has all the heart and stamina you could ask for and we'll stand a grand chance of winning."

"She'll do all right, but what about you? It's a hard ride under the best conditions and after making such phenomenal progress it would be foolhardy to attempt something that might set you back."

"I can do it, Dad, honest. Riding's easier than walking for me now, and they allow from seven to eight hours to cover the sixty miles. You've *got* to let me do it. I won't stand a chance for the scholarship if I don't. It's too late to try anything else under Point Three. Why didn't you say so earlier if you wouldn't let me enter?"

"I thought you might change your mind or think of something else you'd rather do. I don't suppose the sky will fall if you don't win the scholarship. I think I can still pay for your schooling."

"But I want singing lessons too! Mr. Minetti says that with proper training I might some day be on the concert stage, but the only good teacher in town is fabulously expensive."

Once Blythe's restraint was cracked, months of pent-up longing made her tell the whole story of her teacher's praise and her own refusal to consider the added expense of lessons, a practice piano, and the inconvenience to the other young Hylands. Blythe's tempest subsided, and, but for the click of silverware and china, silence ringed the table.

"Why didn't you tell us earlier, hon? Why not let your mother and me decide? Maybe we could have figured out some way."

"That's what I didn't want you to do. I know we're sailing pretty close to the wind and if you were spending a lot of money on me, it wouldn't be fair to all the rest of you—nor the ranch, and that has to come first."

"I suppose Blythe could tell whether she was getting too tired and drop out," Mrs. Hyland suggested softly. "You wouldn't be foolish enough to go on when you knew you should stop, would you, dear?"

"Of course not. Dad, please let me."

His expression softened as he looked at the eager girl, sparkling with vitality.

"Let's leave it this way. We'll talk with Dr. Harrison and if he says it's OK, it's OK with me."

"Yippee, he will, I know he will. I'll get some grain after school tomorrow."

Dark Sunshine could probably not have told, had she been asked, that there was any difference in her routine except for the fact that she saw her adored friend mornings as well as after school. Mr. Hyland fed her some grain the minute he reached the corrals and as soon as she had cleaned it up, he turned her out to be ready for Blythe's whistle.

Before the conditioning began in real earnest, Dark Sunshine was fitted to her first shoes, for up until then her own flintlike hoofs had been tough enough. They were so hard, in fact, keeping them shaped had been a real chore for horse and trimmer. Blythe hovered anxiously around the itinerant blacksmith who came to fit "baby's first shoes" as she called them. The smith was kind and patient and the mare sensible about the strange doings, so it was accomplished without incident except that Superdog made himself sick eating too many hoof parings.

Blythe confined their morning periods to slow work, much

of which was up and down the nearby knobs, or a fast, flat-footed walk through the sandy stream bed that cut across the home pasture. Hours and hours of walking grew monotonous, however, and the girl hit on a scheme for making the time doubly valuable. While doing her homework at night she outlined each lesson on a card which she slipped into her pocket the next morning and, as the buckskin stepped off the miles, Blythe reviewed the day's assignments. By this device the time spent on Dark Sunshine's training became more of an asset than a liability. From time to time Blythe carried with her the poems and passages she had to memorize and the mare had every opportunity to appreciate the works of Shelley, Keats, Wordsworth, Shakespeare and others.

"You'll be a 'high school' horse for sure before I'm through with you, Sunny," she said one day as she dismounted.

Blythe slapped the golden rump that was beginning to show the taut muscles beneath it. The hackamore was slipped off and the mare wheeled and trotted to her favorite grooming ground where she rolled and scratched with many a satisfied grunt.

"It's a good thing you can curry yourself so well, girlie. It sure saves me time."

After a day at school Blythe welcomed faster work. Dark Sunshine did too, and she rarely failed to shake her head jauntily when the pace was first stepped up. Trotting became easier and easier for the girl and became a regular part of the training routine though the mare's rocking-chair lope was unequaled for comfort.

With the thought that she might have to make weight Blythe added a pair of saddlebags but even this addition of several pounds affected the mare not in the least. Blythe watched her horse like a hawk and never saddled or unsaddled without checking the feet, legs, back and girth line to detect any possible soreness or irritation.

"You're a stout one, Sunny, and I hope you stay that way. The only thing that might keep me from entering was thinking it might harm you. So take care of yourself, yes?"

The warm jacket Blythe had worn on her first early morning rides gave way to a lighter cotton jacket and then that too was discarded as the passing weeks took her into a hot, southern spring. Dark Sunshine easily absorbed all the work Blythe could give her, including increasingly long week-end rides, thereby presenting another problem.

Going into the last few weeks of school Blythe's work was immeasurably harder. Regular classroom assignments were difficult enough but the extra work that she had set herself practically doubled her preparation time. It required browsing through the library to find the supplementary material she needed, then once found she must read it and correlate it with the regular lesson. Yet Dark Sunshine's training must go on except for an occasional day's rest to keep her from going stale.

Blythe was so rushed every minute she hardly had time to consider her two-edged problem but she mulled it over in the back of her head. Going home in the jeep one day, the answer jounced to the surface. The trip to and from school was waste time since it was too rough and too windy to study. Why not ride Sunny instead? It was high time that the mare became accustomed to sights and sounds she would never experience at the Lazy SL.

Maggie had often urged her to ride in for a visit and use their extra stall. Dan could meet her there with her school clothes and the trio could go on to school as usual. Fifteen miles morning and night would be an ideal workout with a nice variety of up- and downhill grades and level going, and a good rest during the day.

"We'll begin by riding in one day and back the next, but it won't be long before we can handle it before and after school. Saturdays I can give her the special work she needs, and Sundays I'll have free for my books. Perfect, huh?" she exulted after telling Dan of her scheme.

"Couldn't be better, Sis. I've been wondering how you were going to find hours enough for all you have to do. I'd help if I could but I can't study for you nor can I exercise Sunny. It all boils down to you."

"Don't worry about not helping. You've done so much already I'm still trying to think of some way to repay you. I will too!"

Clipping off the miles to town became a pleasant duty and a dutiful pleasure that put Blythe in fine spirits for the day ahead. Dark Sunshine also profited by the change of scene and watched her new surroundings with interest. For the first few days Blythe was satisfied with going directly to and from Maggie's, but then she began making short detours through the town.

Dark Sunshine's astonishment when she saw her first train was comical as it was less fright than curiosity, and Blythe went out of her way to introduce the mare to strange sights and sounds. As she became more accustomed to traffic Dan was instructed to drive Shasta past them at a great rate, the horn blaring wildly.

Whatever the added attraction the pattern of their ride remained much the same. It began with a fast walk that Dan once clocked at five miles an hour, followed by an extended trot which Blythe had come to enjoy as much as did her horse. After another walk that carried them over the first ridge they picked up the canter Blythe counted on for making distance, followed by another walk, a trot and then a long walk to cool the mare before stabling.

Shasta, too, proved of inestimable value, as in compound low Dan was able to coast alongside or behind in order to make suggestions for improving Blythe's riding form.

"I've read that good balance and proper weight distribution are the secret of success in long distance rides," Blythe told him, "so be sure to tell me when I seem off center."

When Blythe felt that her life was packed as full as one life could be, she was reminded of the riding club's annual gymkhana which had been completely erased from her mind by more pressing affairs. It was to be held the second Saturday in May and, even though Saturdays were devoted to Dark Sunshine anyway, Blythe had had other plans. Nevertheless, riding club standing was too important to risk skipping their yearly event.

One fact made it worth while, for Dark Sunshine had never been around more than one or two strange horses at a time and Blythe was willing to change her plans in order that Sunny might benefit. Attired in her best riding clothes, the tack shining thanks to Chris's energetic ministrations, Blythe

set out from the Lazy SL early Saturday morning in order
to lunch and rest at Maggie's before the show.

So slight a departure from her schedule had put Blythe in
a festive mood and, even though she planned to enter only
one or two events, the afternoon's activities beckoned invitingly. She hummed as she rode. Came the canter and Sunny's
hoofs struck the notes of a bold, rhythmic tune Blythe had
never heard before. They sang themselves over and over until
she found that they fitted the words of a Browning poem she
had recently learned in English.

"Boot, saddle, to horse, and away, rescue my castle before
the hot day brightens to blue from its silvery gray. Boot,
saddle, to horse, and away!"

The music died away at a walk nor did it fit the trot, but
the canter's cadence was perfect accompaniment and Blythe
felt feverishly in her pocket for pencil and paper. No luck,
she had cleaned up too much. Certainly she couldn't hold
Sunny in a canter the whole way, and Blythe closed her mind
to everything but the melody until she rode into her friend's
yard.

"Maggie, let me have a pencil and paper quick. And bring
your English book too, will you?"

Maggie stared at her wonderingly.

"Come on, quick, before I forget."

"All right, all right, but it does seem as if you could forget
your home work today. 'All work and no play,' you know."

"It's not that. I've just thought of a wonderful tune for a
song, and you know Mr. Minetti asked each of us to turn in
an original composition. This's a corker."

Blythe sang it over once as she jotted down notes and rests, and Maggie too was captivated by the air and they sang it together as they rode to the gymkhana.

"Sh-h, don't breathe a word of it here," Blythe cautioned. "I want to surprise Mr. Minetti."

Dark Sunshine required all of her rider's attention then as, head up and tail arched, she pranced and curveted to show off before all the other horses. The girls circulated freely to give Sunny every opportunity to grow accustomed to the milling mobs of girls and horses. Rounding a corner of the stables they were nearly blinded by a silver-rigged palomino and his equally bedecked rider.

"Good grief, Rhoda. Wearing all that hardware I'll bet you need a block and tackle to get on your horse," Maggie exclaimed inelegantly.

"Oh, hello, Margaret. Isn't it beautiful? My daddy gave it to me for my birthday. Why, hello, Blythe. I see you *do* ride. What events are you entering?"

Blythe's mouth opened to reel off all kinds of events—speed and handiness, stock horse, anything that would wipe off Rhoda's patronizing smile—but common sense saved her.

"I'm not riding in much, just the grand entry and I guess the apple eating contest and maybe something else. I don't want to take any chance of getting Sunny stove up. We're entering the endurance ride in a couple of weeks."

"*You* are!"

Rhoda's inflection, intentional or not, changed an ordinary exclamation into an insult direct. Maggie puffed up like a bantam, but Blythe was amused.

"Yes, *I* am, Rhoda. It takes quite a horse to beat a tough

little buckskin, you know. Come on, Maggie, it's 'most time to start."

"Why couldn't Dan like Maggie instead of that bunch of affected fluff," Blythe wondered silently. "Guess he can't see past the frosting on the cake."

The rest of the day passed uneventfully and, while Blythe and Sunny won no prizes, the girl felt well rewarded by her horse's ready acceptance of so many other horses and excitement. She was interested and curious, but she did not burn up her nervous energy in useless fretting. If either of them did it was Blythe, for casual as her first reaction had been to Rhoda's barb, the points hurt and they worked in deeper and deeper.

XIX: Without a Leg to Stand On

BLYTHE HAD plenty of practice ignoring public opinion during the days that followed, for as soon as endurance ride entries were announced and all Red Rock learned that she was planning to ride, anyone who had ever sat on a horse felt qualified to pass an opinion on her chances. Some considered it fantastic and said so. More thought that Dark Sunshine could be a winner with a different rider, and still others believed in both horse and rider.

The girl was much too busy to listen to any of them, however, and plunged into the last two weeks with Spartan determination. Final examinations were but ten days distant yet she must keep Dark Sunshine at the peak of condition. Monday, Tuesday and Wednesday she rode Sunny to school as usual but Thursday and Friday she eased off and rode her only a short while in the evening, every other minute being devoted to her books.

Scholarship candidates could almost have been picked out by walking through the halls and marking the girls with the tense, withdrawn expressions and Blythe was no exception. By that time it was difficult for her to honestly evaluate her chances. Music she had few doubts about and felt sure that her composition would net her the highest mark. Geometry was a safe A, thanks to Dan, but only once had she been able to make an original contribution toward the plus that she coveted.

Literature and History would be the deciding factors and everything hinged on the finals—whether Blythe had absorbed and correlated the extra work she had done to such purpose that her papers might be masterpieces of facts, their back-grounds and explanations presented with a clarity and under-standing that would impress her teachers. In moments of optimism Blythe felt like a veritable Hyland encyclopedia. At other times her brain felt wooden and she despaired of making even an A.

Saturday morning she put her school cares resolutely be-hind her. This was to be a "Sunny day" and she happily dressed in her jeans.

"I'm going to put up a lunch, Mom. Sunny and I will be gone all day, and don't worry about me if we aren't back until late this aft.

"Chris, where's that old canteen I saw kicking around a while ago? I'm likely to be a little thirsty and I don't share

Sunny's enthusiasm for the water holes. Might get my feet muddy."

"Want me to come along, Sis?" Dan inquired, a sparkle in Blythe's manner telling him something was up.

"No, thanks, Dan. It'd be dull for you. Sunny and I are just going to dog along and see what we can do. You might put a feed of oats in the saddlebags for me, though, if you've got time on your hands. She'll get hungry too."

Blythe rode down the driveway and stopped to wave before turning east. Horse and rider were occasionally visible on the long, white road before it curved out of sight around a distant hillock—the same spot where they reappeared hours later. They grew larger by the minute as Sunny's ground-eating stride carried them toward home.

"Whew! That was quite a work-out," Blythe greeted Dan when he met her at the corral. "Here's a place you can sure help. Sunny's got to be cooled out extra carefully and given a good rubdown."

"You too, I should think, Butch." Dan shot a keen glance at her. "You look a little peaked in fact. Go on to the house and I'll look after your mare."

"Oh, I'm all right except for being a little tired. I'll just sit here and give you the benefit of my advice and moral support."

Blythe smiled as she sank wearily to the ground, and she stuck it out until her horse had been carefully cooled, groomed and stabled, but Dan noticed that Blythe walked heavily on her crutch when they went to the house.

"Boy, me for a hot bath and bed as soon as we have supper."

"Lucky it's Saturday night, eh, Butch? The bathtub will be right handy."

They laughed at the Hylands' standing joke about their "bathroom." Blythe was true to her word and was in bed before the last sunset flame died, only to be up early the next morning, her books spread out before her.

Monday Blythe rode in the jeep again since her mother and father planned to meet her after school for the appointment with Dr. Harrison that was to decide whether or not she could participate in the endurance ride. Her folks had wanted to make the appointment earlier but she had demurred on the grounds that it couldn't be a fair decision until just before the ride when she too was in tiptop condition.

"Now don't you talk about it until I'm back in there—or else leave the door ajar," she chuckled after the doctor had completed his examination. "The defendant is entitled to speak for herself, you know."

"All right, young lady. What do you have to say in your defense?" Dr. Harrison asked as soon as she rejoined them.

"Just this: it's only a sixty-mile ride and we're allowed a minimum of seven hours, a maximum of eight hours to complete the distance. Speed is no more important than the horse's condition at the finish and it's all judged on a point system. There's a lunch stop and rest of an hour and, as a matter of fact, any contestant can stop to rest along the way so long as no forward motion is involved. Barring accidents, I know I can do it, so please do agree with me, Dr. Harrison."

"That sounds like a long grind. I've no doubt you could do it, but can you do it without any ill effects?"

"I'm *positive* I can—and maybe win too!"

"That's a large order. How can you be positive about an unknown quantity?"

Blythe hesitated, only to take a big breath and rush on.

"I'm positive I can, because I already have. Saturday Sunny and I did just about the same number of miles within the allotted time—and I'm here to tell the tale."

"Don't bother answering, Dr. Harrison. That's deliberate disobedience and for that—"

"Wait a minute, Dad. Wait a minute. That's not disobedience at all. You said I couldn't enter the endurance ride without Dr. Harrison's OK, but you've never said anything about any other riding. All I did was take an extra long ride, most of it right on our own Lazy SL. So what's wrong about that?"

Blythe held her breath to see how her father would take it. The expressions that flashed across his face—anger, chagrin, discomfiture, almost a paternal pride—made his wife burst out laughing.

"Take some of your own medicine for once, Ty. If that isn't you all over again. You've been out-maneuvered."

Dr. Harrison's deep chuckle joined the chorus when Mr. Hyland's face relaxed in a small-boy grin.

"All right, we'll skip that, but what I said still goes, Blythe." He salvaged what dignity he could from the ruins. "You can't enter the real ride unless Dr. Harrison says it will be all right."

"But that leaves me without a leg to stand on," the doctor began, only to shoot a guilty look at Blythe who hadn't noticed his figure of speech. "She proved she can do it, but quite apart from that the improvement she has made during the past months verges on the miraculous. If horseback riding is responsible—and from what you tell me it must be—I'd say let her ride to the moon if she wants to!"

Shasta led the pick-up into the Lazy SL's backyard where they found "Also" Russell waiting in his car, a truculent Superdog circling it stiff-legged with many a low growl.

"That dog of yours has the shortest memory I ever knew. In spite of the fact that I had dinner here a short while ago and he put his head on my knee so lovingly, today he told me in no uncertain terms I'd be better off sitting in the car. What a watchdog!"

"Yes, he does take his duties a little seriously if no one is at home. He'll be all right now though. Come on in," Mr. Hyland urged their wary caller.

"I can only stay a minute. I came to tell you, Blythe, that I'm glad you're riding in the endurance ride too. I sure hope you win—if I don't."

"You'll have to step pretty lively, Mr. Russell," Blythe answered lightly. "That Sunny mare of mine is quite a go-er."

"She certainly is. And another thing, if I can help you any with your arrangements, count on me. For instance, how about my trailering her in for you the afternoon before the start? We all have to be checked in and the horses stabled at the rodeo grounds for the vet's inspection by five o'clock."

"Oh, that would be a life-saver! I've been wondering how I'd get her there without using up a lot of her ginger. I've wanted to tell you how glad I am that I'll have a friend in the ride. Now I'm extra glad!"

"Also's" visit was short and he had no sooner stepped in his car than Blythe grabbed her books and shut herself in the bedroom for the rest of the day, taking only a short break

for supper. One factor was in her favor. Dark Sunshine's
training had hit its peak during the preceding week and she
had only to be kept in top form. Monday after their dress
rehearsal ride Blythe had given her only an early morning
walk.

Tuesday she rode her to town for the last time, but her
mind was less on her mount than the impending Honors Assembly which was, in effect, a final totaling up of extra-curricular achievement.

With a modest satisfaction Blythe reviewed her past year's
accomplishments: her song with appropriate rewording had
been adopted officially by the riding club; glee club and triple
trio with solo; class officer; treasurer of the First Aid Club
(at Maggie's urging and the indisputable argument that some
day it might be vital at the Lazy SL, Blythe had joined only
to find herself elected treasurer); contributor of occasional
feature articles to the school paper.

The brightest feather in her cap, however, was having been
the moving spirit in founding and becoming first president of
the school's current events club. It had all grown out of a
Hyland discussion at Christmas time when Chris had wanted
to turn off a commentator for another program.

"No, Chris, please," she had objected. "I want to hear him.
We were discussing that very point in history when class
ended and I need fresh ammunition for the next go-round."

"Aw, what's the use listening to that stuff? We can't do
anything about it!"

"Not now, of course, but when we can, we'd better know
more of what's been happening than will show in the daily paper. We're living a big chunk of history right now, and when

you're grown up you'll wish you could remember more about it."

Her words had come back to her during the next current events forum in class. On the spur of the moment she suggested the formation of a larger group, one to take in the whole school, and the idea had gathered size and momentum like a flood tide, sweeping her in as presiding officer. The whole movement proved to be so successful the principal had decreed that next year one assembly a month should be devoted to panel discussion of current problems to be led by none other than founder and first president, Blythe Hyland.

The girl shivered a little at the prospect but consoled herself by the intervening months. At least, she thought thankfully, win or lose she'd have more time next year. "Win or lose" brought her back to her surroundings and the end of dawdling or she would be late.

Honors Assembly was a formidable procession of classmates being presented with an imposing array of honors, Blythe found, but what cut the deepest was the awards of school letters to many of the scholarship aspirants. Even winning the endurance ride would lack the dash, the glamor of having a double R to wear, but Blythe somehow managed to shrug it off. At least she was still in the running so far as other requirements were concerned.

The next day, Wednesday, finals began and that night Blythe frantically tried to review everything she had studied all term but, whether or not she learned anything in those last feverish hours of study, they seemed to calm her and give her confidence, so that she was able to face her coming ordeal with a sort of quiet desperation. She had done the best she possibly could and if another girl was better, she deserved to win.

The atmosphere around the Lazy SL ranch house was super-charged throughout the examination period. The radio was never turned on and when Blythe was studying the others spoke in whispers, walked on tiptoe. Each night she came home with blue smudges under her eyes that almost matched the ink stains on her fingers, but Dark Sunshine was not the only one in first class shape. A night's rest erased Blythe's fatigue and made her ready, almost eager, for the new day's ordeal.

Her last examination was Friday morning and that noon, walking out of the big front doors, she could barely restrain a series of wild "Yippees," but when her mother asked how she had done she only shrugged philosophically.

"Everything is relative, Mom. It's not just how I did but how the others did too, but this much I know. I hit 'em hard and did my best. Now I have to win that ride tomorrow!"

XX: *Last Star I've Seen Tonight*

WITH THE singleness of purpose that had been Blythe's from the beginning and had helped her to rivet her attention on the immediate problem, she put all thoughts of her finals behind her and her partnership with Dark Sunshine became all-important. "Also" had promised to come for the mare about three-thirty that afternoon and the Hyland team leaped to have girl and horse ready.

Blythe saddled the mare and walked her around for perhaps fifteen minutes to limber her up. Dismounting by the corral where her helpers, Dan and Chris, waited, she laid her head against the mare's cheek in their only ceremony.

"Next time I ride you it will be the pay-off, Sunny. I hope I can do as well as you deserve."

"Of course you will, Butch! Don't give it another thought. Come on, let's get busy."

Chris took the saddle and bridle for a final cleaning and, putting all his heart and plenty of elbow grease into the operation as well as generous amounts of saddle soap, he achieved results that were beautiful to behold. Constant cleaning and soaping had blended the saddle's different shades of leather and they were as soft and pliable as a kid glove. Not content with mere soaping, Chris undid each buckle, and wiped and polished it so that not one bit of dirt remained.

"You must have second sight, Dan," Blythe commented as she watched Chris's soulful devotion to his work. "One of those magazine articles I read on long distance rides said that a Mexican saddle is the perfect type, that it keeps the rider's weight forward instead of throwing it back toward the loins where so many stock saddles do—and that's what gives a horse back trouble."

"Sure, I read it in the stars one night myself," Dan grinned. "With your bright saddle blanket it doesn't look half bad, does it?"

"I should say not, but I love it no matter how it looks. It's as comfortable for me as it is for Sunny—but I'd ride bareback if I thought that would help. Some riders have done that, you know."

Dark Sunshine was their assignment and she was curried and brushed until her body gleamed like cloth of gold, her black points shone with the luster of ebony. Blythe's arms were tireless as they brushed and combed the fine, full mane and tail that cascaded about the neck and flanks in gentle waves. Her foretop fell forward across the broad forehead and her eyes almost twinkled as they peered out beneath her bangs.

Blythe picked up her hoofs, one after the other, cleaned them out with a pick. She tested each new shoe to make certain it was tight and true and that there was ample clearance between sole and ground as protection against stone bruises.

"Looks like she's as ready as she'll ever be," Blythe finally commented. "Guess I'd better put in a few licks on myself now."

Mrs. Hyland, however, had been busying herself with Blythe's preparations and had a bag packed with clean clothes for the ride and such toilet articles as she would need for her night's visit at Maggie's. It had been agreed that Blythe should ride in with "Also" and the horses. Dan was to come in very early the next morning in order to feed and groom Dark Sunshine and give Blythe a send-off, while the rest of the Hylands would be waiting for her at the finish.

"Wish me luck as you wave me good-bye," she sang with pretended gaiety from her position beside "Also," once Sunny and all her equipment had been loaded.

"Next time we meet it'll all be over—for better or worser."

There was a chorus of good-byes and good wishes, which included "Also" as well, for everyone from Amy to Mr. Hyland liked the Russells—and the car pulled away. Blythe relaxed against the cushions, but her mind refused to ease up. Heretofore she had felt most confident of acquitting herself well in the ride, in fact, she had been counting on a good showing there to bolster her other accomplishments, but suddenly her thoughts turned traitor and she was amazed at her temerity. How could she ever hope to win over such stalwarts as "Also"?

Yet win she must. There was all the money her father had

spent for Dark Sunshine's extra feed. Unless she won, how
could she repay Dan the entry money she had borrowed from
his hard-earned hoard that was earmarked for a fancier car.
Above all, there was the scholarship that was so important to
her, that might alter the course of her whole life. Her knuckles
whitened as her two fists tensed with determination.

"These long distance rides are unique in one respect,"
"Also's" voice broke in on her turmoil as he intended it should.
"I can't think of a single other sport in which everyone, from
youngsters like you to oldsters like me, can enter on equal
terms. Can you?"

"That's right, there's nothing like them." She pondered this
truth which soon led her to another. "And there certainly
isn't any other event that I could enter with everyone else
and have an even chance of winning. That makes it doubly
wonderful!"

"Also" had ridden in previous rides and he shared his
knowledge with Blythe, so that she felt like a veteran when
the trailer pulled into the rodeo grounds on the outskirts of
town and stopped by the stalls allotted them. Luis, "Also's"
foreman, had been there for some time and had the stalls bed-
ded deep in straw, two water buckets for each horse and
everything that might add to equine comfort.

Dark Sunshine and Golden Go were unloaded and buffed
a little brighter for their appearance in the arena with all the
other entries, when the official veterinarians would examine
them for pre-race defects. With Sunny's halter shank in one
hand, her crutch under the other arm, Blythe started for the
ring.

"Luis can lead your mare for you if you'd like," "Also" offered helpfully.

"Oh, no, thanks. I want Lady Luck to think I'm right in there trying!"

"What are you going to do about your crutch tomorrow, Blythe? It'll get to be sort of a burden if you carry it with you."

"I'm not going to bother. Dan can have it ready for me when we stop for lunch and I won't need it on the trail. I'm one contestant they won't have to worry about making any 'forward progress' when dismounted, but if I do get off I can hop around without it."

From every aisle other entrants were converging on the ring and their horses ran from one end of the color scale to the other: blacks, browns, bays, chestnuts, pintos, grays, roans, an apaloosa, palominos, and another buckskin. Before the actual inspection the officials were introduced to the contestants and their friends and the judge summarized the rules.

"The start is seven a.m. sharp. The route is a big loop leading out of town to the west and swinging around in a semicircle to the old Roger Ranch for the lunch stop. That, as you all know, is just a few miles from here, and many of you will wish you could take it as the crow flies and come home, but the trail goes on for twenty-five miles more before it turns back, and the home stretch is right down that road out there." He pointed to the one that led to the Russells' ranch and the Lazy SL.

"Each rider starts with 120 points from which will be deducted time differences (too fast or too slow) and your horse's condition at the end. Every horse will be checked at the lunch stop as well as here at the finish. In addition there will be observers spotted along the trail to note each horse's condition— and to make sure that the conditions of the ride are fulfilled.

"More than anything else I want to impress on all of you, any criticism that such rides as this get comes from what is sometimes called 'horse killing.' Any official is entitled to disqualify any horse at any spot in the ride, but rather than this if you feel that your horse is tiring unduly and reaching a point where it is detrimental to the animal, I urge you to voluntarily withdraw in the interests of good sportsmanship and the good name of the ride.

"No doubt you are somewhat interested in the prize money. Perhaps I should not mention it now lest it make you too eager tomorrow, but here it is: the purse with entry fees added totals $1,450, of which $704 goes to first, $456 to second, $200 to third and $90 to fourth. And good luck to you all," he concluded smilingly.

"If I can only win the ride and the scholarship, I'll give the money to Dan for his car," Blythe thought desperately. "It's not the money but the recognition I'm after, and we're going to get it, eh, Sunny?"

At first the buckskin had been on tiptoe from excitement but as the inspection went on and on she quieted down and when Blythe limped over and sat down in the dirt, her back to the wall, Dark Sunshine slouched beside her. At long last the trio of judges reached them and Dark Sunshine was subjected to minute examination. She was pressed, pushed, felt of all over until Blythe became uneasy at the prolonged attention, but the veterinarian's words changed her mood to joy.

"So far as I can make out, your mare is absolutely sound.

Are there any defects you know of that you wish to claim in advance lest they become aggravated during the ride and are subtracted from her score?"

"No, I don't know of any," Blythe said thoughtfully.

"It's amazing to find a horse of this age without a single blemish."

"Well, she never had a rope on her until she was nearly five and I've been extra careful of her ever since. I'm the only one who has ever ridden her," Blythe added with quiet pride.

"You're to be congratulated on her excellent condition. You two ought to make a good showing," the man said in parting.

"Also" and Golden Go soon cleared the judges and the two horses were returned to their stalls. Then Blythe realized just how tired she was. She willingly accepted Luis's offer to look after Sunny as well as Golden Go while she rode to town with "Also." Maggie was waiting on the front porch when they drove up and Blythe found herself receiving as much care as a racehorse—a good dinner, a hot bath and even a back rub which Maggie promised would make her sleep soundly.

"Don't worry about waking up in time. Both mother and I are setting our alarms and we'll have you up in time for breakfast. By then Dan will be here, so you just take it easy. Good night—and no dreams at all to you!"

Released from her book worries, Blythe fell into deep slumber instantly and seemed not to have stirred throughout the night, but a habit of many months' standing is not easily broken and Blythe awakened before her call. Feeling refreshed and ready she nevertheless stayed in bed and tried to relax. Through the window she could see the sky paling as the sun drew nearer. A solitary star hung above the western horizon.

"Star light, star bright, first—*last* star I've seen tonight," she corrected herself, only to stop short lest it mean she would be last.

Two alarms tinkled only seconds apart elsewhere in the house. Blythe squeezed her eyes shut an instant while her whole body and mind fused in one big wish. Then she scrambled out of bed humming "Boot, saddle, to horse, and away!", and was almost dressed before Maggie opened the door.

"You're a sneak to get up before I told you you could," she accused. "You may need those extra minutes of rest pretty badly before the day's over."

"Not me! I feel like a million. If the doctors could patent anything as wonderful as a good night's sleep, it'd be worth a fortune," Blythe chuckled. "You look as if you could use several hours more yourself."

"Yeah, I didn't sleep very well," Maggie admitted sheepishly.

"Jiminy, Dan mustn't have slept at all. Here he comes now." Blythe's last words were hardly necessary as Shasta proclaimed her advent before she was even in sight.

"Lucky for you there isn't a Noise Abatement Committee in Red Rock or you'd be on the spot," Blythe greeted him. "You and Shasta are sure 'murderers of sleep.'"

"Not today, Butch. The whole town's up. At first I thoug'.c there must be a fire but I guess everybody and his brother are up to see the ride start."

"Sure they are," Maggie agreed. "There'll be hundreds

there—maybe thousands. Red Rock really takes this ride seriously."

"The bigger the victory, my dears," Blythe imitated Red Riding Hood's wolf. "How's Sunny, Dan?"

"Fine and sassy and rarin' to go. So's Golden Go. I snooped around the stalls to look at the horses and I wouldn't be surprised but 'Also' is the man to beat."

XXI: Boot, Saddle, To Horse, and Away!

HORDES OF PEOPLE were already converging on the rodeo grounds when Blythe and her two helpers drew up at the stable entrance, but Dan expertly maneuvered Shasta right up to Dark Sunshine's stall.

"You take it easy for a while, Sis, while we get your mare in shape. No use wearing yourself out with a currycomb so early in the game."

For a time Blythe was content to sit in the jeep and supervise proceedings, but the air of excitement all around soon made it impossible for her to sit still. She clambered out and with one of her Christmas rub rags wiped off the black and gold head before slipping the hackamore into place. This was checked at every point of contact to make sure no needless irritation would result.

Dan groomed the mare quickly and efficiently, and at a nod from Blythe the saddle blankets were set in place with infinite care. To make sure that no hair might be brushed the wrong way the blankets were first placed slightly forward on the withers and gently slipped back into proper position. Then the saddle was lifted and laid on top in one soft, firm motion and the girth tightened.

Blythe reached down for Sunny's front leg and, lifting it, pulled it slightly forward. Then the other, to draw the loose skin out from under the cinch.

"I guess that's it. How about a leg up today, Dan, to make sure I don't rough up her back hair?"

Blythe set her left foot in Dan's cupped hand, his other was braced against her shinbone for balance and she lit in the saddle like a bit of fluff. Her knees pressed Dark Sunshine forward and, Dan and Maggie walking beside her, Blythe headed for the ring and her great adventure.

Thirty-seven riders out of thirty-nine entries lined up for the start and the horses represented every light breed known, as well as many of mixed or unknown ancestry. "Also" and several other acquaintances spoke to her but Blythe could spare little more than a bare nod of recognition she was so intent on the starter and his assistant. The enthusiastic spectators were entirely outside her ken and once Dan and Maggie had faded into the background only her horse, the starter and herself seemed real to the white-faced, resolute girl.

Something dimly familiar pierced her fog of nervousness

and the feeling grew stronger and stronger. In a flash her mind opened up and she recognized her own song, "Boot, saddle, to horse, and away!" A quick look at the stands disclosed a large percentage of glee club members who waved to her as they sang and all her agitation dissolved in a warm rush of gratitude for her well-wishers.

At that instant the gun cracked and a wave of thirty-seven riders swept forward. A few brash ones left at a canter but the cooler heads, Blythe's among them, merely stepped forward in a warm-up walk. Their way led around the track to the far gate and the shouts and cheers of the spectators followed them across the open space and out onto a dirt road.

Blythe sat her saddle easily and swayed to Dark Sunshine's walk that even that soon began proving its worth, for one rider after another was overhauled. By the time the mare had warmed into her long stride she and Blythe were up with the leaders of the slower contingent and only the half dozen reckless ones were ahead.

For the first hour the line-up remained very much the same and Blythe walked and trotted when the others did. One of the front riders fell back and stayed with Blythe's group during most of the second hour while they traversed the broad valley, but as the road rose to the top of a ridge the first burst of speed began to tell and he was overtaken by the next group.

Sunny stepped along effortlessly and their hours and hours of hill work showed results in her easy breathing at the top of the grade. There the trail swung right and rose and dipped as it followed the high places northward. This up- and downhill travel in the third hour began to take its toll and three more of the leaders were overtaken while two of Blythe's group lagged and those remaining were strung out over a quarter mile of trail.

Blythe used every art of horsemanship at her command to save her mount. Occasionally she rode the stirrups to relieve saddle pressure on the buckskin's back and, rather than insist that she take the hills at a snail pace, Blythe permitted Dark Sunshine to pretty much pick her own gait.

The mare's long stride, both at the walk and trot, ate up the ground with a minimum effort and pressed the other riders who would keep up with her. Blythe rubbed Sunny's satin neck in encouragement and a brown eye rolled in answer.

The girl had expected that the two leaders would have fallen off the pace by then, but they apparently were still going strong. Perhaps she had underestimated their horses. She looked at her watch. One hour to the lunch stop. She must overhaul them by then in order to complete the first half on an even basis, and she was confident that Dark Sunshine had ample reserves left.

They picked up a trot which the girl posted carefully to minimize her impact with the saddle. The riders ahead understood her intention and also began to trot, yet Blythe was unruffled and maintained a steady pace. The distance began to lessen as Sunny outmatched their horses, stride for stride, nor did Blythe draw rein for two or three minutes even after the leaders dropped back to a walk.

The mare was given a chance to ease her breathing and Blythe's heel again touched her into the trot. The fore riders

were less anxious to imitate her and the gap was closed by
half. Blythe looked behind and rejoiced to see that she was
about halfway between the leaders and her former com-
panions. The flash of a golden horse told her that "Also" had
taken her place, that his methodical progress was showing results. Her throat tightened as she recalled Dan's words,
"Maybe 'Also' is the man to beat," but her hand was steady.
This was Sunny's turn to walk. Anyway her own muscles
began to beg for relief.

The mountain ridge was petering out and Blythe's eyes
scanned the country below for the welcome rest spot. Once
she realized how tired she was her right leg began to grumble
until she finally had to humor it and drop her feet from the
stirrups. She leaned forward on the horn to distribute her
weight and the periodic jabs of the pommel served as a counterirritant, making her glad to slip her feet back into place.

The mare was sent into another trot and her rider was soon
able to distinguish more minute details about her rivals ahead
before the trail turned around a sharp outcrop of the moun-
tainside. Girl and horse hurried on and, when they too had
cleared this corner, Blythe found one of the riders standing in
the trail, his horse blowing heavily. Her first surprise turned
to understanding when she recognized the animal as one of
the most poorly conditioned horses in the event.

Blythe acknowledged the rider's greeting but rode on, her
heart sorrowful, not for the rider but for his overworked
mount. She wondered fleetingly how it had held up that far,
but her attention soon shifted to the one contestant between
herself and the lead.

"We'll just go our own gait, Sunny. Maybe he'll have to ease up too and save us the work of overtaking him."

Her hunch was a good one. The leader seemed to have lost his drive and the distance grew less and less, eaten up by Dark Sunshine's steady progress. Blythe was so engrossed by her duel with the leader she forgot those behind until the thud of hoofbeats turned her in the saddle. "Also" nodded sociably.

"Looks like the Russell horses are right up there, doesn't it?"

"They sure are, and it won't be long 'til they're in front. That horse up ahead has lost all taste for this business."

Blythe's words were prophetic and on the next level stretch the pair trotted smartly past the tiring leader. Challengers were in sight by then and buckskin and palomino were urged into their fastest walk until the descent grew steeper. Then they walked on the downhills and trotted on the level, if only for a short distance, until the trail lined out across the valley floor. Far ahead through the heat haze they saw the clump of trees that meant lunch and rest, and their followers were as far behind.

"How about a lope? Think your mare's up to it?"

"I'm sure she is—and I've been dying to rest myself with a lope for miles. There'll still be time to walk 'em in, won't there?" Blythe asked.

"You bet. Those trees are farther away than you think— not that the horses will have much chance to cool out in this heat—and we can take 'em in in good shape."

Palomino and buckskin swung into an easy canter that nevertheless widened the gap between leaders and followers

at every step. The pair drew rein when their lead had been
protected and side by side, as though they were on a bridle-
path, they rode into the welcome shade.

Dan's satisfied grin as he reached for Sunny's reins was
his only comment. Not so Maggie whose chattering was as
excited and unintelligible as a telegraph key's, but her actions
made sense. She had brought an air mattress for Blythe to
stretch out on and insisted that Blythe lie down, but Blythe
refused to do so until Dark Sunshine's inspection was complete and Dan was capably tending to the horse's needs.

Only then did the hot, tired girl sink down and only then
did she fully realize how much more wearing competitive
riding is than a solo ride. Without a word, Maggie pulled off
the right boot and gently massaged the weaker leg. She wiped
Blythe's hands and face with a towel dipped in cool water
and let it rest a moment on the back of her neck.

"Now just close your eyes for a few minutes before you
eat lunch. I'll keep everyone away."

That was not too easy, however, and many well-meaning
but thoughtless people would have spoken to the girl had it
not been for watchdog Maggie who, finger to lips, insisted
on silence. Blythe stirred within a few minutes and sat up.

"I do believe I catnapped a little at that," she said in surprise.

"Course you did, and it's the best thing in the world for
you. Now how about lunch?" Maggie chirped. "Here's your
favorite sandwich, an orange, and some hot tea—"

"Hot tea! On a day like this? Have a heart. I'm not sure
I want anything."

"Oh, yes, you do! Just a little fuel in your tank will keep

you going, and 'a tired rider makes a tired horse,' you know."

Blythe watched the crowd while she ate and decided that a majority of the morning's crowd had come out to the half-way stop. Once she thought she caught a glimpse of Mr. and Mrs. Forbes, and through an aisle of people she did see Dr. Harrison who sauntered over. Not a detail of Maggie's house-keeping set-up escaped him and his twinkle grew brighter.

"Well, I guess you must be a Girl Scout, young lady," he approved before turning to Blythe. "Good going, Blythe. How do you feel?"

"Not bad, Dr. Harrison, not bad. Like about twenty-five miles more."

"All right, but don't forget your promise. If you get too tired you'll pull out. By the way, I hope you have your poncho. Looks like our summer rains might be early this year." He nodded idly at the masses of whipped cream clouds that reared up from the valley's eastern ramparts.

"That I have, right on the back of my saddle, and if it'll rain on our range too it can come any time."

A few minutes remained of the allotted time and Blythe and Maggie drifted toward Dan and the buckskin who seemed to have bounced back with as much resilience as her rider. The sweaty coat had been sponged off and brushed back to its former luster and a light feed of grain and sparing sips of water had restored much of her energy. This time Blythe was content to merely supervise the saddling and bridling though she couldn't resist one tweak at the saddle blanket.

She and "Also" mounted and waited for the timer's signal which gave them a twenty-minute start on the next group.

At his "Go" they rode away from the shade into the hot, dry valley. The last lap. The home stretch. Blythe scanned Golden Go for any telltale signs that might mean Dark Sunshine had the advantage, but find them she could not. It was still anybody's race.

XXII: The Fork in the Trail

WELL, THERE are five less riders for us to worry about," "Also" observed. "One was disqualified and the other four dropped out back there."

"Is that so! That's encouraging—except they probably weren't the ones we'd have to worry about anyway. How many had come in?"

"All but three, but of course the ones that rode up just before we left are hardly competition. We have nearly an hour's advantage."

"Good, let's keep it and have another little lope while we're still in flat country," Blythe suggested. "Seems like the farther ahead we can get now, the better."

"Also" agreed and the two horses rocked along in a classic canter, the most enjoyable part of the day for their riders.

Alternate walking and cantering took them, in surprisingly
good time, to the foothills where the going was easier than
the morning's terrain had been. They skirted the foot of the
mountains, crossing one undulating swell after another while
overhead the billowing clouds kept pace with them. To the
riders' relief the sun was blotted out although they could
see that its brilliance was undimmed on the other side of the
valley.

Blythe reached behind her and loosened the ties on her
poncho at the first big spatters but "Also" was less cautious
and waited to see what might develop. The cool wind that
breathed gently on them was equally welcome to horses and
riders and seemed to instill new energy in them all.

"Here it comes!" Blythe snatched her poncho as a gray
curtain swept down from the mountain and enveloped them
in a rush of rain. "Also" yanked frantically at his raincoat
and finally managed to undo and shrug into it just as the last
drops fell. The two looked around in astonishment to see the
squall driving northward along the valley, leaving bright
sunshine behind.

"Shucks! That much rain was hardly worth the effort,"
he laughed. "Now I just have to do it up again."

"Me too, but every drop was worth its weight in gold to
us. The rain will lay the dust and soften the footing for the
horses and it has freshened up the air wonderfully. See, they
agree with me too."

Dark Sunshine and Golden Go did lift their heads and
seemed to drink in the cool freshness that followed the little
rainstorm, and this made their riders willing to forget their
damp spots. The first hour ended with both pairs as fresh as

they had been on leaving the halfway point, but Blythe began to puzzle about their situation.

They couldn't just ride on together all afternoon or it would turn out to be a dead heat, yet neither would it seem very nice of her to try to forge on ahead. Probably if she did, "Also" would move Golden Go along faster too and they might wear each other out and allow some other rider to win. She wondered whether similar thoughts were troubling her companion during his long silences.

Blythe pondered this possible stalemate, but Golden Go himself gave her the tip-off when her ear caught the click of steel on steel. He was getting leg weary and careless in his step. She half closed her eyes and strained to catch any irregularities in Dark Sunshine's pattern but heard only the regular one-two-three-four of her walk. Surely her mare would have more speed and stamina left for the finish if it came to a dash. Then too, if Golden Go was forging, there might be telltale marks on his hoofs and legs that the keen-eyed vet would see and grade accordingly.

"Also" too seemed to be tiring, just how much Blythe could judge from her own aching muscles that cried out for relief yet rejected any shift in position as inadequate. Nor did the girl dare try many changes for fear of tiring Dark Sunshine, the more important member of the team at the moment.

Their way curved right and led up into the mountains by an abandoned mining road and Blythe forgot her other problems in easing herself and her mount during the ascent. Twice they stopped to breathe the horses and once the top was gained the two riders agreed on a ten-minute, dismounted stop.

From their lookout they scanned the country behind for

competitors. At first it seemed barren of life except for a hawk that circled lazily below them, but Blythe's quick eye spied a moving dot on the lowest foothill and pointed it out to "Also."

"We didn't gain as much time as I'd hoped. Can't be more than half an hour behind us—but that grade will keep him in his place," "Also" said with supreme unconcern. "Look this way, Blythe, I'll show you something even better."

She followed the direction of his finger and down on the other side of the mountain range she was astonished to see Red Rock itself.

"But it seems so close. We can't be that near the finish!"

"Don't get your hopes up, we aren't. Remember the judge said we make a big loop around town. This is just about the nearest point. There's a side trail that leads off down near the bottom and if you're getting too tired, this'd be the best place to drop out."

"Oh, I'll be all right."

"Well, in case you're ahead of me at that turn-off, don't take it or you'll be disqualified."

"I'll remember," Blythe promised lightly, "but I don't expect to be ahead and if I'm behind I can follow your tracks. Time's about up, isn't it? Don't want that upstart behind to catch us."

Blythe hopped up on a little rise to mount Dark Sunshine and the two riders took the down grade with new hope to allay their fatigue. The horses too seemed to know that the worst was over and pressed forward. Evidently the rainstorm had been heavier on the heights and from time to time a hoof skidded off course a few inches although the horse recovered easily.

More than anything else the absence of conversation proved how tired the riders really were and the descent was carried out in total silence but for the squeak of a saddle, the jingle of a bit and the palomino's forging. The trail became too narrow for two abreast and Blythe drew rein to let "Also" ride in front. From this position directly behind Golden Go she could appreciate how very leg weary he was and she thought she could see twin spots on the inside of his fetlocks where he clipped himself from time to time.

Blythe became almost hynotized by the rhythmic back-and-forth motion of the palomino's white legs, until she was completely oblivious of the trail ahead. Apparently "Also" was equally unwary and did not see the black rope that slithered down the bank and into the trail before him. Quicker than sight it whipped into a coil and the air vibrated with a sound like a hundred tiny seed pods shaken by a wind.

Golden Go's reaction was instantaneous. His front feet left the danger zone and he stood straight up on his hind legs to pivot away. Instead of sand or gravel underfoot his off hind hoof struck a small patch of clay wet by the rain to the consistency of grease, and the horse crashed sidewise like a felled tree.

Riding in a fog of weariness, "Also" had perhaps one second's warning of impending disaster. He flung himself free of his horse, his arms outspread to cushion his fall, but he struck heavily on the edge of the trail and rolled five or six feet to the bottom of a tiny wash.

Blythe snapped out of her daze. In the middle of a step

forward she pulled Dark Sunshine back in time to escape being carried down by Golden Go's momentum. Her right leg flashed over the horse's back and the girl flung herself to the ground in one lightning motion.

"Never let a rattlesnake get away!" rang in her ears. She scooped up a handful of rocks and showered a stony rain on the loathsome pile in the trail. Several struck their target and Blythe kept up the bombardment until the snake was mortally injured.

Only then did Blythe turn her attention to "Also" who, she had half expected, would join her in the attack, but he lay where he had fallen. She spared one wildly anxious look up the trail though she knew their pursuer could not catch up for fifteen or twenty minutes, and that might be too late. Then she crouched and skidded down the incline.

Blythe knelt beside "Also," recalling no scrap of the First Aid she had learned at school, but to do something she took an arm and turned him on his back. About to feel his legs and arms for broken bones, she saw a spot of vivid crimson on his upper sleeve. It grew larger with every heart beat. A cut artery!

With trembling hands she whipped out her jackknife and slit the sleeve from wrist to shoulder, baring a jagged wound where his arm had crashed down on a sharp rock. Blythe bit her fist in near panic and while she did the crimson stain spread.

"Stop it, I've got to stop it someway! A tourniquet, yes, that's what the teacher said, a tourniquet to stop the bleeding."

Reason and coolness returned with the thought and she

yanked loose the bandanna she wore around her neck. Her hands flashed as they folded it into a flat bandage which she wrapped around the man's upper arm.

"Now a stick. Gotta have a stick," Blythe chattered, looking around her frantically, but only old, dead wood offered itself. She lunged for a bunch of greasewood and cut a stout section which she slipped through the double knot. She twisted rapidly, and her own heart seemed to hang motionless as she watched for effect. One or two more spurts stained the bandanna redder before the pressure began to tell and slowly, grudgingly the pulsations ceased.

She fastened down the ends of the stick to maintain tension, then fanned his white face and rubbed his forehead. As though her touch recalled him from where he had been, "Also" opened his eyes.

"Just lie still, 'Also.' You're hurt a little, but you'll be all right. That other man will be here in a little while, but *be sure and lie still.* I'm going for help."

Before mounting Blythe pulled out the notebook she had always carried since the day she made up the song. She scribbled a hasty note which she tucked under the stick on "Also's" arm, telling the next comer to loosen the tourniquet immediately and if the bleeding had stopped to leave the bandage loose.

The man's eyes were closed and Blythe shouted as though they were many yards distant instead of a few feet.

" 'Also!' " He opened his eyes sleepily in reply. "Hang on, 'Also.' Don't go off again. I'll try not to be long."

Dark Sunshine knew little of their changed plans, but that something was altered she could tell from her rider's changed tactics. Forgotten was all thought of saving her mount—only speed mattered. The whole incident had taken perhaps five or six minutes, Blythe thought, but it seemed like an hour and she pushed her horse down the trail recklessly, intent on but one thing.

The mare stumbled once and this jarred Blythe back to reality, replacing one turmoil with another. She remembered the grueling miles behind them. Her heart pinched as she thought of the ordeal still facing the mare.

"Can you do it, Sunny? You've got to! If you don't—" Her fingers twined in the soft mane, caressed the thrusting shoulder already harsh and crusted with sweat. "You'll just have to do it, Sunny. It may be his life against—" A sob choked her.

A few turns below Blythe found the fork in the trail. Not until then did her own sacrifice confront her. It was not just a fork in the trail. It might be the crossroads of her whole life.

"Don't take it or you'll be disqualified."

"Also's" warning jangled through her head and the magnitude of her decision shook her. If she turned off she would lose the ride, the scholarship, the money she wanted for Dan. Her entire year's work would be wasted, perhaps her whole talent, for how else could she ever attain singing lessons. A convulsive tug on the reins stopped the tired buckskin. Maybe she could finish the ride and still get help to "Also" in time! The bleeding had already been stopped and other riders would be coming up.

She nodded her head and reined Dark Sunshine into the longer trail. Three steps were all the mare took before her irresolute rider checked again. Suppose the bleeding started up when the tourniquet was loosened? There might be broken bones, too, or a concussion. "Also" had to have a doctor. Dark Sunshine was turned around and her hoofs found the short cut.

"I can't do it, Sunny. If he died it'd be just as if I had killed him. How could I ever sing again, knowing that? Come on, we've got to hurry!"

The few seconds' delay weighed on Blythe's conscience like hours, and she urged the mare onward. She was surprised to find how direct the steep side trail really was, for after a few minutes' riding it leveled off into foothill country. With no thought of her own safety Blythe urged her horse into a canter and, rocks and dirt flying in every direction, they raced downhill. Far across the white plain she could see the trees and buildings that meant Red Rock. How far? she asked herself desperately. Five miles maybe. Maybe less.

Blythe tried to push Dark Sunshine on, but their rapid descent and continued speed left little reserve strength. The girl yanked at the knot that held the short length of hackamore rope. For the first time in their friendship the buckskin felt the sting of a lash as her rider fanned the lathering flanks.

This startled the mare into a faster gallop and they rocketed along. Once Dark Sunshine stumbled terribly and Blythe rocked precariously, but she clung savagely to the saddle. Buckskin though the horse was, she had no yellow streak in her and Blythe knew that she would gallop until she dropped. The girl hoped that they might intercept a car on the road and cut short their mad run by a mile or more, but not one was in sight.

"Just a little ways, girlie. Keep it up. Keep it up. Keep it up," her mind said over and over with the thundering hoofs that she was to hear in her nightmares for weeks afterward.

Again the mare stumbled and Blythe's heart bled at the punishment her darling was taking but every second counted. They tore through the fringes of Red Rock, turned one corner and raced down the home stretch.

XXIII: Blythe and Sunny

IT's BLYTHE and Sunny," someone shouted, and, echoing the cry, the crowd surged forward to greet the winner. Mr. and Mrs. Hyland and Dan were in the forefront, but Blythe's frantic gaze swept across them blindly as the staggering buckskin shambled to a halt.

"Dr. Harrison! Where's Dr. Harrison? I want a doctor. Dr. Harrison! Dr. Harrison!" she called into the milling mob.

"Get off, hon, and tell us about it. What's the trouble?" her alarmed parents cried. Blythe scarcely heard them.

"Dr. Harrison. Come here quick!" she called, seeing him push through the crowd.

"Here I am, Blythe. What's the matter? Get down and let me look at you."

"Oh, it's not me. It's 'Also.' " Blythe gasped out the story and every other word was "Hurry!" Before she was half through men sprang into action. The place was easily identified by the turn-off and a jeep was commandeered for the rough return. It was loaded with necessary equipment—blankets, medicines, a stretcher—before four stalwart men and a doctor jumped in and sped away.

"Well, you seem to be the winner, young lady. Please dismount so we can check your mount," a sober-faced judge told Blythe.

"No, I didn't win. I took the short cut. I'm disqualified." Her voice shook at this admission, and—the need for haste past—she felt dazed, uncertain of what to do.

"Come on, Blythe. I'll help you off," her father said gently. "Your Sunny needs to be looked after."

Truer word was never spoken, for the gallant mare's labored breathing racked her from nose to tail. Her head drooped to her knees and rivers of sweat ran down every leg, dripped from her belly, her fetlocks, blackened her hoofs as though she had forded a river.

Mr. Hyland scooped his daughter into his arms and lifted her down like the baby she had once been, but when she saw her horse's pitiful condition Blythe kicked and squirmed to get free.

"Put me down. Put me down. I've got to look after Sunny. She's got to have good care or she'll die. Let me alone." Her voice rose hysterically and sobs punctuated her words.

"Take it easy, hon. The vet's right here. He knows just what to do and he'll pull her through. Just see if he doesn't."

"I'll stay with her too, Butch," Dan promised. "I'll look

after her just the way you would. You go along and get a little rest."

"That's right, Blythe. You come with me." Dr. Harrison's kindly face swam into her ken and Blythe's eyes widened with horror.

"Dr. Harrison! The jeep's gone. Hurry, take another car. You can still catch it. Hurry. Hurry!"

Blythe verged on frenzy when it seemed that her efforts had been vain, that the jeep had gone off without the doctor. She squirmed out of her father's arms, but her numbed legs could not support her and she would have crumpled in a heap had Dr. Harrison not caught her.

"Easy, Blythe, relax. Dr. Schaeffer went with the jeep. I stayed here to look after you," he soothed. "Come on, I'm going to take you off where it's quiet so you can get a little rest. Yes, your mother and dad are coming too."

"But Sunny? Will she have good care? I oughtn't to leave her. Where is she?"

"They've taken her to her stall, Blythe, and I'll guarantee you that that mare will have the best care that this town can provide. Nothing's too good for a horse like that! From now on if you want to ride her with golden horseshoes, she could probably have 'em."

Dr. Harrison strode to his car, Mr. and Mrs. Hyland following in his wake through the path that opened up like magic in the respectful crowd. Afterward Blythe was never sure whether she actually remembered being taken to the local hospital where she was fed lightly and put to bed in clean, cool sheets or whether she had reconstructed it from her parents' story.

She did remember clearly waking up the next morning with a ravenous appetite which the nurses delighted in satisfying. Dr. Harrison looked in while she was reading the Sunday paper and he was delighted by her bright-eyed appearance. He took her temperature, blood pressure, listened to her heart which delighted him the more.

"Well, young lady, I didn't really give you my permission to turn heroine, but it looks as if you're none the worse for it."

"I'm no heroine. Sunny did it all. How is she? Is she—?"

"She's just fine," he said heartily, ignoring the unspoken fear. "Here're some folks who can tell you better than I can."

Dan and Maggie entered, not knowing just how to act, but Blythe's joyous greeting was their cue.

"Hi! How's Sunny? What'd they do for her? Does the vet think she'll be all right? Will I be able to ride her again?"

"Whoa, Butch. Sure, Sunny's coming along just great. About as well as you are, I'd say. She's up this morning, moving around her stall a little though she's kind of stiff, but her appetite's good. Boy, did she lose weight, but there's no cause to worry at all the vet says," Dan summarized rapidly.

"Jeepers, Blythe, are you the stuff in Red Rock!" Maggie caroled. "See that cloud there over town? It's made up entirely of 'Blythe Hyland,' 'Blythe Hyland.' Maybe you didn't win their old ride but you showed 'em you could have."

"I didn't though, and that's what counts on the scholarship." Blythe's gaiety trickled away, as she measured her loss impersonally. "Oh, well, what's an old scholarship anyway?" she said with a transparent attempt at casualness.

Neither Dan nor Maggie had to be told what it meant to

her and they were silent, wondering what to say. Again it was Blythe who took the lead.

"The nurse told me this morning that 'Also's' doing all right. He's still pretty weak from loss of blood but except for that there aren't any serious injuries. 'Contusions and abrasions' I believe covers everything else. He had to have a transfusion last night when they brought him in."

"Yeah, I know he did. I was just going to ask how he is today," Dan said.

"How'd you know he did?" his sister demanded. "You were supposed to be looking after Sunny."

"I know 'cause Dad was here when they brought 'Also' in, and Dad gave him the transfusion. That's how I know."

"Well, what d'ya know! Looks like the Hylands are still a team, doesn't it?"

Dan and Maggie soon returned to Sunny, their other patient, and Blythe was left with her own gloomy thoughts, but not for long. A nurse stopped in the doorway.

"Another caller, Jerry Kennedy. Shall I send him in?"

"Yes. No, no, wait a minute. How do I look? Should I comb my hair again?"

The nurse looked at her critically, punched up her pillows, smoothed the covers.

"You look just right, especially with that pink blush veil you're wearing. Now?" she teased softly.

"Yes, now."

Blythe looked up casually when footsteps paused in her doorway, but Jerry was so combed and slicked she hardly knew him. One hand held a box of candy, the other a bouquet of roses, and he looked as though he'd come straight off a

Saturday Evening Post cover. This gave Blythe an inner chuckle and instantly put her at ease.

"Hi, Jerry, come on in and sit down."

"Here," he said as though relieving himself of an onerous burden. "The candy's from me; the roses are from Mom."

"They're lovely, but she doesn't even know me."

"Now she does. Everybody does. How're you feeling, Blythe?"

"Topnotch, but they can't seem to fill me up. Let's open the candy."

Breaking the seal broke the ice and they gobbled and gabbled busily. In a short time Jerry looked like his comfortable old self, and felt like it too.

"There's a dance at Rec Center Tuesday night right after Commencement, Blythe. How about staying in with Maggie and going with me?"

"It wouldn't be nice to go off and leave Maggie like that," Blythe hedged.

"Who said you'd be leaving her? She and Dan are going too."

"They are! I thought he was going with Rhoda."

"No, he decided she's too stuffy—Maggie's more his style."

"Just what I've been wanting to tell him," Blythe nodded happily.

"Then you'll go with me?"

"I didn't say that at all. Maybe I won't even come in for Commencement."

"But you have to. That's when the scholarship's to be awarded and every candidate has to come."

"Well, I'm not going to win it, so what could they do to me?"

"Ah-ha, my proud beauty, but you have to sing with the glee club—or they'll bounce you. How'd you like that?" Jerry knew that he had scored that time.

"Don't count on me for the dance, Jerry. You'd better ask someone else."

"We-ll, maybe. I'll see you at Commencement anyway, won't I?"

"I suppose so," Blythe agreed shortly, hurt in spite of herself that he seemed willing to take her suggestion.

Jerry soon left with an airy farewell, but Blythe had little time to brood as her mother and father came to take her home. On the way they drove past the rodeo grounds so that Blythe could see for herself how Dark Sunshine was doing, but returning to the scene of her high hopes that had fizzled to a dud was cold comfort. Wordlessly she held the mare's gaunt neck in her arms a moment while her heart said a prayer that no permanent damage would result.

Blythe found no solace at the Lazy SL, for every place she looked reminded her of her tireless work either in conditioning Dark Sunshine or working for her extra high marks. That she had succeeded so well only to fail in the pinch was the ultimate in irony, and she drifted around the ranch despondently.

Losing the ride meant losing the scholarship and it meant that she could not present Dan with her winnings in return for all the fine things he had done for her. It also presented an acute, more immediate problem. So sure had she been of winning she had borrowed the entry money from Dan's little hoard and now she was faced with finding a way to repay him. Her mind whirled from one sore point to another, piling bitterness on bitterness. The only consolation was that "Also" was recovering nicely.

"Don't take it so hard, hon. Your mother and I will find a way to see that you get those lessons. Fact is, I think I know just the ticket."

Blythe looked at her father's cheeriness with dull, lifeless eyes. She knew her parents shared her disappointment and wanted to help.

"The money you've saved for our indoor plumbing, I'll bet. That's no fair. I won't do it that way."

"Not necessarily. Might be we'd get another windfall," he disclaimed, but she could tell from his guilty look that was exactly what he'd had in mind.

"Don't worry about me. It's just sort of lonesome without either Dan or Sunny here. Tomorrow'll be better."

But when Monday brought her brother and her horse somehow it only seemed to make her feel worse. Seeing them made her accuse herself anew, because of what she had done to the one, and what she hadn't done for the other. At least it gave her a locale for her brooding, a wailing wall, and she spent hours sitting in Sunny's corral, watching every movement she made, attending to her slightest want.

The abrupt transition from being frantically busy to having nothing at all to do aggravated her dejection and hours spun out like days. Books she had laid by, eagerly awaiting vacation leisure, seemed too dull to bother with, and when she looked at her accordion her throat tightened up and she wondered whether she could ever sing again.

Mr. and Mrs. Hyland had been determinedly cheerful but by Tuesday they too were feeling the strain and, when even Chris's exuberance ebbed, the Lazy SL became a passable imitation of a morgue. Dan was more miserable than his sister, if this was possible, and he could find no way to comfort her. He tried every subject that had ever interested her, even topics that had chirked her up briefly during her illness, but they died of their own weight.

Blythe's mother adopted a bold approach Tuesday noon when no mention had been made of the evening's activity.

"Come on, Blythe, I can help you wash your hair now so it'll be soft and pretty tonight."

"I don't know as I should, Mom. Look at my throat, will you, and see if it's red. It feels kind of scratchy." Blythe cleared her throat very convincingly. "Maybe I oughtn't to try to sing tonight."

Mrs. Hyland took a clean spoon and gravely peered into the mouth her daughter obligingly opened. Pink it was, yes, but not red.

"I don't see a thing there that our little surprise for you won't cure."

She waggled Blythe's jaw tenderly in her hand. Mrs. Hyland paused slightly but sensing there would be no reaction, she hurried on.

"A new dress, Blythe. A party dress for you. It's just perfect—you'll look and feel like Miss America."

"You folks shouldn't have done that. I don't need a new dress. I hardly think I'll go tonight. I guess you can probably return it though."

"You can guess again, Blythe Hyland! You're going and

you're going to wear that dress, so you can decide now
whether you want to have clean hair or hair with all the dust
and perspiration of the past week in it."

Mrs. Hyland's dander was up and Blythe read the storm
warnings. Her father she could frequently jolly out of his
tempers which blew up like thunderstorms on hot days, but
when her mother got her pressure up it meant a real blow.

"All right. All right. I'll go and look like a ninny."

"You won't do any such thing. Some girl is going to win
that scholarship and my daughter is going to walk up to her
and congratulate her. Then if you want to tuck your tail
between your legs and scat for home, you can."

"We-e-l-l."

"Well, yourself! Besides, you know 'Also' sent word he
wants you to stop in to see him in the hospital tonight before you go on to the high school. Now, do you want me to
help you wash your hair?"

"Yes, please," Blythe answered meekly, vaguely comforted
by the old-fashioned treatment.

XXIV: Bonus

WE'LL WAIT here for you, Blythe," her father decreed when the pick-up stopped in front of Red Rock's hospital. "Better not stay too long though. We're a little behind schedule and you don't want to be too late to sit with the glee club."

That's exactly what Blythe would have liked but after her mother's earlier explosion the girl dared not say so. She passed the lighted hospital desk and walked down the darkened corridor, feeling that the place held out sheltering arms to her. She longingly remembered the sanctuary of her own bed there and wished fervently for a sudden attack of something, anything, that would prevent her attending the high school's ceremonies, but she had not been stricken by the time she reached "Also's" door and tapped.

"Come in," he boomed so jovially Blythe forgot she was visiting a sick man. "Well, it's good to see you looking so fine," he greeted her.

"That's my line," she smiled. "You took the words right out of my mouth."

"Oh, I'm all right. Should have been out of here long ago but that doctor's sure a stubborn cuss. Whatever happened to me was my own fault. Served me right for not being wider awake, but you, you might say, went looking for trouble. I've heard about that ride of yours down the mountain. It's a miracle you weren't killed."

"Also" was silent a moment and Blythe opened her mouth to give Sunny the credit but he plunged on.

"I know as well as everybody else that you saved my life the other day. It's a funny thing too. I'd been sticking along with you to kind of look after you. Figured as soon as we hit the home stretch I could outsprint you, and then the whole thing backfired on me."

"That is funny," Blythe admitted, "because that's exactly what I had figured. I was kind of worried there for a long time, the cozy way we were riding together, until I decided it was nice to have company and that when we got to level going I'd shake Sunny on and beat you. As easy as that!"

In spite of all she could do to keep the conversation light there was a somberness in her voice she could not cover up.

"Sort of figured you had that race won, didn't you, girl?"

"Yes, I kind of did there toward the last. I thought Golden

Go was tiring faster than Sunny—that she'd show him her heels at the finish."

"That's exactly what she would have done. It's a lucky thing for me that you weren't riding Golden Go, or I'd have lost—for keeps! As it was, you'd have won if it hadn't been for my boner, so I want to make it up to you. Here."

He thrust a slip of yellow paper toward her, but her arm remained at her side.

"Thanks for thinking of it, but I don't want anything. If it hadn't been for you I'd never have had a horse to ride for help. If you think I ought to be paid, I already am, paid in full."

"You are not. You've just admitted before witnesses," he nodded at his wife who had just entered, "that you thought you had that race won so here's a check for the same amount as the winner's purse. Doesn't that sound reasonable?"

"Not really—you don't owe me anything," Blythe reiterated.

"Let me tell you, young lady, my life means a lot more to me than this check does. If you don't take it, you'll put me to all the effort of going out and looking around and then probably buying something you don't want and wouldn't have on a bet. So you'll save us all a lot of fussing around by taking this check."

"Go ahead, Blythe. Take it! I can tell you 'Also' never does something unless he wants to," Mrs. Russell urged, "nor will he be put off doing something he wants to do. If you don't take it, you'll likely wind up with a diamond tiara or a white elephant."

"Which will it be, this or a white elephant?" "Also" demanded fiercely.

"All right, I'll accept it on one condition. Tear that one up and write out another to Dan Hyland. I'd intended to give him my winnings to buy a new car."

Blythe's spirits lifted a little at the prospect of squaring her accounts with Dan. Money could never pay her debt to him, that would take her a lifetime, but she could repay him the loan and help him toward his heart's desire. Her eyes sparkled at the pleasure he would get from a better car.

"Sure I will, but that's pretty generous, isn't it?" "Also's" words brought her back to her surroundings.

"No, I don't think so," she said softly. "If it hadn't been for Dan I might still be dragging myself along on two crutches. That's *my* life, if you want to look at it that way and, as you said, it means more to me than figures on a check."

Mr. and Mrs. Russell twinkled like Mr. and Mrs. Santa Claus as one check was replaced by another, but while Blythe's heart was happy that Dan would be taken care of, her mind was heavy with the prospect of her coming ordeal. Nevertheless she waved cheerily to the Russells as she went out the door and, once the Hylands joined the stream of people entering the high school, Blythe was in too strong a current to resist.

She smiled and talked and laughed with her friends but as her zero hour drew closer she wished that she had braved her mother's wrath and stayed at home. Now there was no turning back. Quicker than thought—her thoughts anyway that dragged along dolefully—the glee club sang its opening number and was seated on the stage. Red Rock's Commencement had begun.

The featured speaker droned on and on in the hot auditorium. Blythe gave up trying to follow his words and strove for a bright, intelligent expression that would make it look as though she were listening attentively. She wished again that her glee club position wasn't in the front row, for tonight of all times she wanted protection from the curious eyes before her.

Blythe glanced down at her lap as if to better consider the truths the speaker was stating and restating, only to be reminded that at least she looked her best in her new dress. It was a love—her first long dress—and she wished she had sounded more grateful. Its graceful folds covered her legs, making her look like anybody else. The color was good too—a soft, warm beige that was very flattering.

It was a good thing she looked nice, she decided, since so many people she hardly knew had come up to speak to her before the program started. She was slightly puzzled by everyone's enthusiasm and approval. Surely they wouldn't expect her to leave a man to die beside the trail.

". . . We can draw out of this bank of life only as much as we put in, and so I say to you, go forward into the future with high hopes and a high heart. God grant they may all be realized."

Blythe joined the burst of applause that greeted the speaker's conclusion. Now the awarding of diplomas and they'd soon be through. She wondered for the hundredth time whether Jerry had taken her advice, gotten another date. She had not seen him until from the stage she had spotted his dark head just a few rows back. She almost looked toward him but, with an effort, fixed her eyes on the superintendent who was reading the honor roll and soon the procession of graduates across the stage afforded her shelter from Jerry's insistent eyes.

"This brings us to the conclusion of the Commencement program proper, but one very important formality remains—announcement of the winner of the Marilyn Forbes Memorial Scholarship. For those of you who may be unfamiliar with the terms . . ." The superintendent's voice went on, explaining what Blythe had lived by for nine months, and her heart pounded so loudly it deafened her to his words.

With all her heart she wished for a position on the back row. She felt her face stiffen and wondered how she could ever manage a genuine smile when the winner's name was spoken, but smile she must and applaud as well. Not a trace of disappointment must show. She geared herself for an instantaneous reaction—smile, clap, nod, look like a good loser. Her face grew tired of the strain of waiting. What in the world was he saying?

". . . talented . . . well liked by classmates and teachers alike . . . a hard worker both in school and out . . . scholarship of the highest quality, 'above and beyond the call of duty,' so to speak. . . ."

Blythe heard the words, but such generalities could apply to any one of the girls. She sat poised for a good loser's reaction.

". . . not exactly the letter of the scholarship but an abundance of the spirit that makes good neighbors and good citizens . . . after thoughtful consideration on the part of the faculty and the donors of this scholarship, who asked me to express their regrets that every one of the fine group of girls could not win, it gives me great pleasure to announce the winner, Blythe Hyland."

So keyed up was Blythe that her hands half met in the time-honored gesture of applause, though to others it looked only like an impulsive clasp of her hands. The full meaning of the words flooded her mind with joy beyond belief, yet she was incapable of motion. Mrs. Forbes had mounted the stage and stood beside the superintendent waiting expectantly. The crowded auditorium throbbed and boomed with noise but Blythe was incapable of motion.

Her neighbor's elbow jabbed her and, rising, Blythe limped slowly across the platform. After Mrs. Forbes had presented her with the envelope that signified success, the audience quieted to hear Blythe's acceptance speech. She half waved the envelope in a salute to her parents and wondered idly why her mother was crying. Even her father looked pretty teary. Blythe turned to Mrs. Forbes and moved her lips soundlessly.

"I—I—I—" she managed on the second try and finished in a triumphant burst, "Th-th-thank you!"

The great orations of history met with no wilder ovation, for Blythe was the popular choice. The hall fairly rocked with noise and a part of Blythe's mind noted that the unsuccessful candidates shared the enthusiasm too—not one seemed to begrudge her the victory.

As the demonstration continued the superintendent spread his arms in a gesture of dismissal and the ceremony ended unceremoniously. By some miracle Mr. and Mrs. Hyland reached Blythe in the first wave of well-wishers and she gave them each a bear hug.

"Mom, what're you crying about? You ought to be happy. I am," Blythe caroled with tears in her eyes.

"Me too, honey! I'm happier than I've ever been. Look what you did in your excitement. Where's your crutch?"

Blythe stared down at herself blankly as though the crutch might be hiding in a pocket.

"I—I guess I left it by my chair," she admitted sheepishly.

"You don't need it any more, sugar. You just thought you did! That's the bonus that comes with the scholarship."

Blythe saw Jerry's curly crest approaching through the throngs. He seized both her hands in his and squeezed them warmly.

"Congratulations, Blythe. You're wonderful—but I've known it all along. Now will you go to the dance with me? You can lean on me for a crutch."

"Oh, will I, Jerry! I've just discovered I don't really need one—but you'll have to remember to twirl me on my left leg."